"I wasn't honest with you about something...I'd like to tell you the truth now."

Lane's voice stopped her when she was just inside the doorway. She was standing on the left side of the threshold; he came to stand on the right.

Cynthia frowned. "What is it?"

"I lied...I haven't dated anyone in a long, long time."

Cynthia's heart began to thump, rhythmically and quickly. He shouldn't have found it necessary to tell her. She shouldn't care.

He leaned towards her again, but this time she couldn't have moved if he'd yelled "fire". "There's something else I should tell you," he said, and pointed up, to the top of the doorframe.

Cynthia lifted her eyes. There was a green sprig taped to the wood.

"It's mistletoe," Lane told her, breathing the words close to her face.

The Twelve Steps of Romantics Anonymous

Step 1.   We admit that we are powerless over romance.

Step 2.   We admit that the search for "true love" has brought chaos to our lives.

Step 3.   We begin to restore ourselves to sanity.

Step 4.   We make a searching and fearless list of our lover's faults.

Step 5.   We read the list aloud to ourselves and to another person.

Step 6.   We make a decision to turn the will of our hearts over to the higher powers of serenity, balance and calm.

Step 7.   In our search for serenity, we come to value Peacefulness above Passion...

Step 8.   ...Reason above romance...

Step 9.   ...and Logic above all.

Step 10. We accept the separation of Rhett Butler and Scarlett O' Hara as unavoidable due to irreconcilable differences.

Step 11. We come to understand that there will be life after romance—for them and for us.

Step 12. Having found peace as a result of these steps, we share our message with other compulsive romantics, and we practise abstinence one day at a time...

For my great-aunt Esther
and my great-uncle Henry—
you put the magic in my childhood. I love you.
And again for Timothy Lane—
today's inspiration.

MILLS & BOON and MILLS & BOON with the Rose Device
are registered trademarks of the publisher.

First published in Great Britain 1998
Harlequin Mills & Boon Limited,
Eton House, 18-24 Paradise Road, Richmond, Surrey, TW9 1SR

© Wendy Warren 1993

ISBN 0 263 81313 4

Set in Times Roman 10 on 12.5pt.
02-9812-46400 C1

Printed and bound in Norway
by AIT Trondheim AS, Trondheim

ROMANTICS ANONYMOUS

BY
LAURYN CHANDLER

MILLS & BOON®

Chapter One

Romantics Anonymous, Step One:
We admit that we are powerless over romance.

"*Can romance be dangerous? Is true love a modern myth? My next guest says yes. Meet Cynthia James, founder of Romantics Anonymous and author of* Love and Marriage and Other Tall Tales *on the next... 'Jack Phelpps Show.'*"

The Jack Phelpps theme music faded out. A peanut-butter commercial came on.

Lane Lincoln stared at his TV.

His hair was still damp from his shower, and he hadn't put a shirt on yet over his jeans. A bagel from Sid's Deli sat on a dish on his coffee table, and he held an opened carton of orange juice in his hand.

It was, in short, too damned early for surprises.

Lane leaned back on his leather sofa and chugged juice from the carton. For weeks he'd been immersed in revisions to his latest screenplay. He'd finally finished late last night and had resurfaced this morning to reward himself with an early-morning jog; the bagel from Sid's, which was the closest he'd come to a real breakfast in weeks; and a trip around the channels just to hear human voices again. He'd had no intention of watching "The Jack Phelpps Show"—until he heard the teaser.

Cynthia James, author, workshop leader...and romance authority. Lane's hand tightened around the juice carton.

In two minutes and thirty seconds Cynthia James would leap onto his television screen and he would have his first glimpse of her in over ten years. Already, her image was filling his mind, unbidden and unwelcome. He slammed the juice carton onto the coffee table. A smart man would change the channel. An even smarter one would turn off the TV. And if he wanted to display unparalleled wisdom, he would cancel his cable and sell the damn set.

Lane Lincoln was no fool. But on this sunny California morning in early December, he violated his every instinct. He leaned forward, reached for the remote and punched up the volume. Then he picked up his bagel, took a vicious bite out of it, sat back again and glared at the TV, waiting impatiently for Jack Phelpps to open the show and introduce Cynthia James Lincoln—Lane Lincoln's *very* ex-wife.

"Hello. Good morning. We have quite a show for you today." Jack Phelpps's face smiled from the screen in a boy-are-you-in-for-a-treat way. "Our good friend Enid Frenlow is here to show us how to make Christmas ornaments we can eat, Rod Marsten will be joining us with hairstyles to boost our holiday spirits and renowned pet expert Forrest Langdon will tell us how to make Scruffy a welcome guest at any holiday gathering.

"But first—" the camera moved in for a medium shot, and Jack modulated his smile "—there's a new book on the stands which suggests that love and marriage—" he shook his head ominously "—may not go together at all." The camera pulled back for a two-shot, and Jack's smile broadened.

"Meet Cynthia James, founder of Romantics Anonymous and the author of *Love and Marriage and Other Tall Tales*. Cynthia, welcome."

Cynthia James looked composed and almost regal with her blond hair pulled into a sleek french twist, her daffodil-yellow suit and pumps perfectly coordinated, and her hands folded comfortably on her lap. Only her smile belied her composure: it wobbled, and she looked unsure of whether to direct it toward Jack or the camera.

Jack pursed his lips and fixed his guest with a serious expression. "Cynthia, your book is a novel, but many people believe that what you've actually written is a treatise on love, sex and romance in the nineties. Do you agree with that appraisal?"

"Well...Jack." Cynthia smoothed one hand down the front of her linen skirt and spoke slowly. "I wrote a novel. You know, it's...fiction...and that's what I intended it to be." She nodded and smiled, then took a deep breath and elaborated when Jack looked like he expected her to say more. "But, of course, my philosophies and my experiences do come into play."

"Ah!" Jack nodded sagely. "You write in some detail about the heroine's first marriage. You're also

divorced, so may we assume that this novel is somewhat autobiographical?''

The question seemed to startle Cynthia.

''Well...'' she cleared her throat when the word
came out as a squeak. ''Excuse me. Well, Theodore
and Lane—I mean, my...Theodore and my ex-
husband are, uh, different. They're two different
people...or, rather, characters.... Or, rather, you
know, one's a person and...and one's a character.''

''But which is which? Right, Cynthia?'' Jack
laughed, and Cynthia smiled shakily at the camera.

''Now—'' Jack held a copy of Cynthia's book in
his hands ''—in the book your heroine, Susan,
leaves her husband, and you seem to be suggesting
that their sexual attraction was not only unimportant
in the long run, but that it was actually detrimental
to their marriage. That's a scary concept.''

Cynthia shook her head and frowned. ''No, it
isn't. I mean, not when you think about it. Not really. I've met with many people in Romantics Anonymous, Jack. And I've learned a great deal.'' She
leaned slightly forward and spoke with increased
conviction. ''A marriage must, above all, be stable.
I think most adults would agree that you can't wager
stability on a hormonal fluctuation.''

''So in your opinion, sexual attraction is just a
hormonal fluctuation?''

Cynthia hesitated for just a moment. ''Oftentimes,
yes.''

''You seem to be taking it a step further, though.''
Jack opened Cynthia's book to a page he had
marked and began reading. '''Susan looked back
across the fields of her memory. In the distance she
saw Theodore. The attraction she once felt was gone

now; it was dust. And looking back, her once trembling passion seemed almost comical.'

"That's pretty strong stuff, Cynthia. 'Comical'? Ouch." Jack hunched his shoulders like somebody had stepped on his toe, then relaxed and smiled again at his guest. "What about chemistry, you know? We all want heat."

Cynthia's face had reddened a bit when Jack read aloud from her book. Now she took another breath and explained her position. "Heat...Jack, is something that is easily created."

"We can create it?" Jack looked interested. "No kidding. Easily?"

"Yes. Look," Cynthia uncrossed her legs and leaned forward. "We can cultivate sexual interest for anyone at any time, and it will be as strong as, and potentially more long lasting, than the feeling that seems to simply pop up between some people." Cynthia's expression grew calmer and her voice became stronger. "Certainly many of us have been in relationships which, when over, left us wondering what we saw in the other person. From a distance, being attracted to them seems almost...ludicrous."

Her eyes flashed, she sat back, and her smile was utterly confident now. "It's a dangerous misconception, Jack, that intense sexual passion is rare, that it happens only once in a lifetime. Or that it's an important ingredient in a marriage. It's just *simple lust*. Chemistry is not the mystery it's been made out to be."

In his Laurel Canyon home, Cynthia's ex-husband wasn't interested in chemistry at the moment. He was interested in finding some ice to apply to his stinging hand. He'd pounded his fist down on the slate coffee table when Jack Phelpps read the part about attraction seeming ludicrous when you looked back. Now he wondered if he'd broken his wrist.

Why the hell did he always realize his mistakes once the damage was already done?

Rising from the couch, his hand throbbing, he strode to the kitchen, growling at the TV. "Damn it, Cynthia."

Lane filled a plastic bowl with ice and stuck his hand into it.

He never should have watched that ridiculous show. He'd made an agreement with himself years ago: As long as Cynthia stayed out of his life, he would forgive and forget her lousy, traitorous, faithless, unwifely desertion of ten years before.

Resting his good hand on the sink, Lane bent forward and acknowledged that he felt, briefly, like sticking his head in a bowl of ice. His temples were starting to ache. Amazing how quickly the old anger, the old hurt, could rear up. It did not please him that in the years since their turbulent divorce, he still hadn't learned to subjugate his feelings to his conscious will. He shook his head and swore again, more softly. "Damn it, Cynthia."

And damn that book of hers.

The book's popularity had first come to his attention last month when a photographer stuck a camera in his face and asked if there were any parallels between Lane Lincoln and "Theodore."

Lane couldn't blame the reporter. Speculating about the author of *Love and Marriage and Other Tall Tales* and her ex-husband, a screenwriter who wrote epic romances, was just too tempting to resist.

After all, his very ex-wife had written a best-selling book about how lousy and useless romance was. Movie rights were being optioned. And she was using her maiden name.

Lane lifted his head and stared out his kitchen window. The last time he'd seen Cynthia she'd been a young woman who dressed in Indian print skirts and bunchy sweaters and carried a baby on her hip—*his* baby. Now she appeared polished, professional, the quintessential career woman. And she was delicately slender again. The last time he'd touched her, she'd had a rounded belly, a tantalizing reminder of the nine months she'd carried his child inside her.

What would that willowy body look like now if they'd stayed together? Would her hips have widened, her body rounded? That would have been fine with him. He would have enjoyed caressing her soft flesh and knowing that her body had changed with time and the bearing of their children.

Lane's hands tightened into fists. "The Jack Phelpps Show" was likely taped a few weeks in advance of the air date. By now, Cynthia had probably visited several more shows and told several more interviewers how "comical" she found her ex-marriage.

He wanted to go back into the living room and glue his nose to the TV.

He wanted to go back into the living room and smash the screen.

Nothing had ever been simple with Cynthia.

He was, thankfully, saved from either action when the doorbell rang.

Lane crossed to the door without looking again at

the television. Wearing only a pair of faded jeans, and without thinking to put a shirt on, Lane reached for the door with his left hand. As he swung it open, he rested his right forearm on the doorframe. His bare torso dominated the entrance.

"Yeah—" Lane's mouth stayed open; his brown eyes stayed wide.

The woman before him was a wreck. Her clothes were wrinkled and her eyes were tired. She looked like she'd been up all night.

"Hello, Lane." Her gaze flicked down as far as the middle of his chest, then shot straight up to his face again. Cynthia pushed a stray hair back from her face and lifted her chin. "I've come to collect my daughter."

Chapter Two

The air in California must be thin in the Hollywood Hills.

That was Cynthia's first thought, and it came because she was experiencing a vague light-headedness as she stood in Lane's doorway in the crisp morning air.

And what a morning it was.

She was standing here, the last place on earth she'd ever thought she would be, nose to chin with her seminaked ex-husband, who was leaning into the doorway like Stanley Kowalski, but with fewer clothes.

One bare muscular arm was resting on the frame just above the left side of her head, and everything that could be exposed legally in public was there for her to see, right down to the line of brown hair that dipped below his jeans.

Not that she was looking.

She, on the other hand, was wearing the rose knitted-wool suit she had worn on two different plane trips in the past twenty-four hours. Her clothes were not, unfortunately, the only part of her that felt wrinkled, and she'd been stuffing strands of her hair back into her chignon for the past hour. It looked like a hairy matzo ball.

Just the way she'd always dreamed of meeting Lane Lincoln again.

Scratch that! She had never even *thought* about meeting Lane Lincoln again. Not once. Ever. And certainly not under the present outrageous circumstances, circumstances which made it very difficult for her to be calm, poised…and indifferent.

Trying to look past him into the house, Cynthia spoke in the steady, professional tone she'd perfected on the last leg of her book tour.

"If you'll just hand over my daughter, we need to be going. You see, we live several hundred miles away and she's late for school."

Lane looked beyond his ex-wife to the yellow cab that was idling in his driveway. He hadn't seen her in ten years, he had no idea why she was here, and she hadn't even told the cabbie to cut his motor.

He leaned more heavily into his raised arm.

Ten years.

By mutual agreement, they hadn't even spoken to each other in all that time. They communicated, when absolutely necessary, through her mother, Lea, or through her sister, Gwen.

He was about to utter the first words he'd spoken to her directly in over a decade. For years, he had wondered what those words would be. He was a writer; he liked big moments and poetic justice. And this was certainly one of life's bigger moments.

Here she was. His very ex-wife.

Ex-lover.

He leaned into her. His jaw tensed once before his lips parted, and his vocal cords got ready. His eyes narrowed. The phone pealed loudly in the room behind him. He pointed a finger at her.

"Don't leave," he grunted, then turned and stalked into the living room, slapping off the TV, where Jack Phelpps had already moved on to Enid Frenlow and her edible tree ornaments.

When he couldn't immediately locate his cordless phone, he headed for the wall mount in the kitchen.

Cynthia watched him disappear through an arched doorway.

He hadn't invited her in, but she crossed the threshold anyway, stepping lightly onto the tile with her high heels. When the taxi had pulled up in front of the lovely Spanish-style home, she hadn't been surprised. After five successful screenplays and a novel that continued to sell well, he'd obviously turned his high-tops in for Italian loafers.

Cynthia glanced around the room. It was attractive. And expensive-looking, in that relaxed but chic, California way. So this was it: his bachelor pad, his swing nest, his party palace. Well, she supposed every Hollywood screenwriter needed one. She thought of her own overstuffed plaid couch (durable for kids with toys), her old pine table with the too-short leg (she'd nicknamed it Captain Ahab), her braided rugs and the old photos lining her walls. Her decor belonged in California no more than she did.

Since she was here to retrieve her daughter, she considered searching the house for Beth, but clicking through the tiled rooms in her high heels while

Lane was on the phone seemed unsavory somehow. Besides, she was too damned tired to move.

All she'd thought about on the plane home from Boston was Beth and how much her daughter would love the pink, Liberty Bell sweatshirt Cynthia had bought her in Philadelphia. The book tour had taken a month, the longest she'd ever been away from her daughter, and Cynthia had been looking forward to nothing so much as being with her little girl again, making Beth's favorite banana pancakes and embarking with her daughter on a school vacation that would also include Beth's thirteenth birthday.

She had walked through her door early that morning, knowing—or rather, believing—that Beth was at a school friend's house, two blocks away. Cynthia had planned to grab a quick shower and then surprise the girls by taking them to breakfast and driving them to school. But before she'd set her suitcases down, the note Beth had taped to the banister leapt out to greet her.

Dear Mom,
I'm not at Sarah's. I'm in California. I'm going to visit Dad. You should probably come get me.

Love,
Beth

P.S. Don't worry. Everything's fine.

Don't worry. Cynthia wasn't even certain she'd locked her door, so quickly had she turned around and run from her house to the car. She'd driven to the airport with dozens of scenarios swirling through her tired mind. She had spoken to her mother the night before. Everyone was fine, Lea had said. Gwen and Franklin, Cynthia's sister and brother-in-law, and their children were visiting from California; they all planned to watch the Jack Phelpps interview together. Bethie was sleeping at her friend's house.

What had happened in the past twelve hours? And why did it involve Lane?

Years of hard-won independence had honed Cynthia's trust in her ability to do what had to be done and to act swiftly. She hadn't for one moment considered *not* getting back on a plane and flying to California, Beth's note and Lane's address shoved haphazardly into her purse.

All right, so here she was. Where was her daughter?

She took another step into the entry.

The phone clicked back into its cradle, and Lane came back into view. He walked through a short, sunlit hallway and into the living room.

Cynthia noted automatically that ten years of gravitational pull hadn't affected him much. He still had ripples in his stomach and clear definition in the muscles of his chest and shoulders. He still wore his sexuality in place of the shirts he shunned.

And apparently he still had that irresponsible, *qué será será* mentality that had wreaked havoc on her heart a decade ago.

Her daughter had disappeared with nothing but a note and he left her standing on his porch while he sauntered off to answer the phone. So typical. Except that ten years ago they hadn't been able to afford a phone.

It was inconceivable to Cynthia that Beth, at age twelve, would have made this trip on her own, without encouragement. Maybe Lane had decided that he wanted Bethie for the Christmas vacation and hadn't thought it necessary to inform anyone. Maybe he had a new squeeze and thought it might be fun to play family over the holidays. Watching Lane advance, Cynthia worked herself into a good lather.

"Where is she?" she demanded without niceties when Lane was before her again.

"When did you notice she was missing?" Lane was standing with his bare feet planted squarely on the floor, his hands on his lean hips. His brown eyes were utterly unfathomable—and she didn't want to make eye contact with him, anyway—but his tone of voice was faintly condemning.

"I found out when I arrived home this morning and found the note taped to our banister." Cynthia struggled to keep her voice even and unemotional even though her jaw was clenched so tightly she had to squeeze the words through her teeth.

"Are you aware that your next visitation is not until Easter and that Beth's grandmother, who is supposed to be responsible for her, has no idea that she's gone? Or that Beth is supposed to be in school today? She has finals in two weeks. Now, I realize that you do things more casually out here in Hollywood—" she let her gaze drop briefly to his bare torso "—but in most of the country taking a child from her home without her guardian's consent or knowledge is considered kidnapping.''

Lane's eyes narrowed, and Cynthia's anger was not eased by his assessing gaze. Her heart was pounding in her chest, the toll of the stress making it skip beats occasionally.

Lane said nothing at all for a good thirty seconds. Then, in the smooth baritone that used to bring goose bumps to her skin, he told her, not unkindly, ''You look like you're about to keel over, Cyn.''

Cynthia turned and hollered into the house. ''Beth?''

''Cyn—'' he began.

''Beth!'' she called more adamantly. ''This is your mother. Come here, please!''

''She isn't here, Cynthia.''

Lane was still watching her calmly, his unreadable eyes unwavering. When he chose not to elaborate, Cynthia folded her arms and stared at the pounded-brass sculpture that hung on one wall.

''Okay,'' she said, lifting her chin and trying not to get a muscle spasm as her shoulders tensed into knots, ''I'll bite. Where is she?''

Instead of answering, Lane looked past her through the door she hadn't closed. ''Why is the taxi still here?'' he muttered, moving to the door.

''He's here because I tipped him handsomely to wait for us. I intend to take my daughter back to Oregon before she flunks the eighth grade.''

Lane turned back to her. ''Tip him handsomely again and tell him to beat it.''

Cynthia didn't move, but a flash of worry sparked her tired eyes.

Lane dug into his jeans pocket. "Okay, *I'll* tip him handsomely."

He jogged out the door without giving Cynthia time to argue. When he came back into the house, he stopped just inside the door.

"If you'll quit glaring for a minute, I'll explain what's happening. Why don't you have a seat?"

Cynthia remained standing.

"All right. That was your mother on the phone. Beth is at your sister's house. She got there about an hour ago."

Cynthia pressed a hand to her chest, an impotent effort to quell the runaway beating of her heart. Gwen and Franklin's home was in Sierra Madre, California, an hour away from Lane.

"Gwen and her family are in Oregon visiting my mother. Beth knows that."

Lane nodded. "But Franklin's mother is there. She called your place, and when you weren't there she phoned Gwen at your mother's." He held up a hand to forestall her questions.

"That's all I know, except that Beth seems fine but isn't giving any explanations until we get there. I'll go wash up and then we'll drive over." He waited for her to say something or to nod, and when she didn't he frowned. "You want something to drink?"

Cynthia shook her head. He started toward his bedroom, and she said, "I suggest you put on a shirt.

Gwen's husband has an eighty-six-year-old grand-mother who lives with them. She's easily shocked.''

Lane's laughter rang off the adobe walls. ''Molly? Who are you kidding?'' He turned to look at her. ''That old gal wouldn't be shocked if we both walked in buck naked. She's seen everything.''

His voice dropped to an intimate, growling caress. ''But since bare men obviously upset *you* these days, Cyn, I'll certainly cover up.'' He winked at her and walked slowly into the bedroom.

Bare men did *not* upset her, Cynthia thought as she sat in the passenger seat of Lane's cherry-red foreign car. Bare men did not, but surprises did.

She knew Lane saw Gwen occasionally when Beth was in California. She knew it, she approved of it, she appreciated it when Gwen acted as a go-between and a buffer. But she'd had no idea that he was on personal terms with Gwen's in-laws.

Gwen was four years Cynthia's junior. She'd been a mere sixteen when Cynthia had met and married Lane Lincoln on a burst of romantic and hormonal optimism. Cynthia and Lane had spent the ensuing four years traveling around the country in a dilapi-dated trailer attached to an even more dilapidated orange pickup.

Their life-style had not given either of them a chance to bond with their in-laws. They had been content to remain a world unto themselves. Or, at least, he had been content.

Lane's blithe confidence had been so attractive to

her back then. Unlike her, he'd never seemed to question his feelings; he'd just had them.

His cocky self-assurance had seemed unshakable...and later, impenetrable.

What had she called it during their last, awful fight? A "paranoiac need to pretend you are in control."

She bit the inside of her lip to keep from shuddering. If there was one thing they hadn't learned from each other, it was the art of subtlety.

In her memory, their relationship was colored boldly, like a Sousa march. It had become very passionate very quickly, and it had stayed that way, almost as if there hadn't been enough room to squeeze in any softer emotions, any sotto voce.

Well, she'd learned the hard way that you couldn't get much depth when there were no tempered moments. Wasn't that what the women and men in her R.A. group discovered time after time until the lessons finally sunk in?

Lane exited the freeway and drove unerringly down the small, quaint streets of Sierra Madre. He pulled up before a lovely craftsman-style home, and wordlessly, they got out of the car. Wordless, in fact, described the entire hour-long drive from Lane's house to Gwen and Franklin's.

Cynthia preceded Lane up the stone walkway and could hear Gwen's shar pei, Zeke, barking up a welcome inside. Before Cynthia could even ring the bell, Gwen's mother-in-law swung open the door.

"Hello, hello. You got here so quickly! Come in, come in."

Lillian greeted them with hugs and an unreserved smile and ushered them into the huge, wood-floored entry. Cynthia hadn't seen Lillian since the wedding, but she felt again the still-familiar warmth the woman exuded and the faintly Yiddish accent that was so appealing.

"Get down, get down!" Lillian shooed as Zeke jumped between Cynthia and Lane, thrilled to have additional people on whom to lavish his abundant affection.

"Och! What can I do?" Lillian shook her head. "So now I'm grandmother and baby-sitter to this seventy-pound wrinkle." She took Zeke's collar and patted him on the folds of his neck. "You want to come into the living room? I'll make tea."

Cynthia smiled, hoping she wouldn't seem rude. "Thank you, Lillian, but I'm just so anxious to see Beth."

"Of course you are, of course." Lillian nodded, pushing Zeke ahead of her and placing a warm hand on Cynthia's wrist before she turned to lead them down the hallway. "You just got back from Boston this morning, Gwen tells me." She clucked her tongue. "The worry you must have gone through."

"We appreciate your calling so quickly, Lillian." Lane said as he walked beside Cynthia. Reaching forward, he placed a hand on Lillian's shoulder and gave it a grateful squeeze.

The older woman reached back and patted his hand with an easy familiarity. "So, what else?"

Cynthia watched the exchange in blooming surprise.

"Beth is in the den with my mother," Lillian continued. "They're watching the TV. We took a cruise to Alaska recently, and my mother had to miss her 'Wheel of Fortune.' Franklin taped the shows so she'd have something to yell at when she got home."

Through the large, arched doorway that led to the den, Cynthia saw her daughter, Beth, and Lillian's mother, Molly, the diminutive eighty-six-year-old firecracker, sitting with their faces glued to the TV.

"Don't spin again. Don't spin again!" Molly yelled in an accent much stronger than her daughter's. She threw up her hands as the recalcitrant contestant bent toward the wheel. "Stubborn!" she declared, shaking her head. She turned toward Beth and raised her still-dark brows. "Two bucks says he lands on Bankrupt."

"Mother!" Lillian admonished from the doorway. "I told you, no betting."

Molly turned and looked at her daughter innocently. "Two bucks. That's such a crime?"

"Come help me in the kitchen. It's time for lunch. Cynthia and Lane are here for Beth."

Molly looked at Cynthia and Lane standing unsurely in the doorway, then turned back to Beth. "So, your parents are here for you. You're not an orphan." She winked. "A girl who takes plane rides all by herself can probably afford a two-dollar bet."

She rose easily from the couch and walked to the door. She smiled at Lane and peered up at Cynthia, whose shoulder she barely reached.

"I saw you on TV today. You put on a good show."

Cynthia, desperate to talk to her daughter, smiled tremulously. "Thank you. I didn't actually put on the show, though. I was just a guest."

"Oh, yeah?" Molly studied her, her head at an angle, her wrinkled eyes thoughtful. Her nod was barely perceptible. "Must be some other program I'm thinking of, then. The woman I saw put on quite a show." She preceded her daughter down the hall, age barely slowing her short, birdlike steps.

Beth rose from the couch and smiled at her parents. "Hi, Mom. Hi, Dad. I'm glad you could come."

Chapter Three

"Beth."

Lane and Cynthia both spoke their daughter's name and took a step into the room at the same time. Their eyes roamed over her, assuring themselves that physically, at least, she was fine. Then Cynthia exercised her maternal right and broke into relieved tears.

Lane turned to her, not knowing what to do, and Beth ducked her head, a little embarrassed, then came to her mother's aid by hugging her happily.

"I'm glad you're back from the tour, Mom. My friend Rachel's mom bought your book. She said you're not nearly as strident in person." Beth smiled like that was a wonderful compliment.

Lane choked back his grin and looked in wonder at his twelve-year-old girl. Her hair was a cross between his medium brown and Cynthia's golden blond, and she had Cynthia's flaxen highlights. The last time the three of them were in a room together,

Beth had been wearing training pants and thought that pressing colored clay into the walls was the most fun a kid could have. Now she was wearing jeans with a label on the hip and preferred to toy with her mother.

He stepped forward and held out his arms.

"I'd like a hug and an explanation—in that order." He smiled at his daughter, and she came eagerly to his embrace.

"Hi, Daddy. You smell like cinnamon and trees. Do you realize I haven't seen you since summer?"

Lane nodded. "I do. Do you realize you aren't going to wiggle out of receiving the lecture of your young life?"

Beth nodded and went to flop back on the couch. "I have a really good reason for what I did, though."

Cynthia couldn't think of a single good reason for a twelve-year-old to fly alone and without consent on a red-eye flight from Oregon to California, so she sat on the couch next to Beth and took her daughter's hand.

"Beth, there is no justification for what you did. It was dangerous and it scared to death the people who love you. If you had a problem, sweet-pie, you could have gone to Grandma, and you know Aunt Gwen is in Oregon right now. You could have spoken to her. You also knew I would be home this morning. There were a lot of different, *safe* things you could have done."

"Not for this problem, Mom."

Cynthia felt her breath catch, and she tried not to make that little "Oh, dear God" gurgling sound she had trouble avoiding in moments of extreme motherly concern.

This was when she felt the burden of being a single parent. This was when every bit of the confidence that usually bolstered her seeped away as though her very blood were draining.

She nodded slowly. "Okay. We've been a team for a long time, kiddo. We can handle whatever it is."

"That's right. *We* can."

Cynthia looked up to see Lane standing behind Beth. He'd obviously said the words while looking at Cynthia, and his expression was angry and grim.

He walked past them, picked up an ottoman and brought it over. When he sat down to face Beth, only loving concern filled his face.

"Okay, Bethie. Hit us with your best shot, kid."

He reached a hand out toward his daughter, but withdrew it quickly when he saw that Cynthia still had Beth's hand.

Beth stood up, disengaging herself from her mother, and paced to a spot where she could face both her parents directly. She stood tall, with her arms at her sides.

She began in a strong, clear voice that sounded to Cynthia like an adult's. "Mother, Father..."

Mother? It was usually "Mommy" or "Mom." The sound Cynthia was trying to avoid squeaked from her throat.

"As you both are aware," Beth continued, "I will turn thirteen in just a matter of weeks. In some cultures, I would be considered a woman at thirteen."

Oh, dear God, Cynthia thought, desperately trying not to squeak again.

Beth turned to pace thoughtfully to the left. "More and more during the past months my thoughts have turned to boys...well, to young men. And then one day I realized, this is it. I'm ready."

Oh dear God, oh dear God! Cynthia screamed in her mind while her supportive smile strained her lips and her jaw locked.

Her hand reached out blindly. Lane grabbed it and squeezed, and Beth turned to face them again.

"You both need to realize that soon, very soon, I'm going to come to you and say, 'Mother, Father...I want you to meet my date'."

"Your *what*?" Cynthia asked through the smile frozen on her lips and the teeth that stayed clenched.

"My date," her daughter repeated. "A boy, Mom. I don't know who he'll be, but there will be one, you can count on that. And I'll need a lot of support, 'cause dating can be frightening."

Cynthia was so relieved that her smile broadened to a goofy, drunken grin and her breath came out in little half-voiced puffs.

Lane released the breath he'd been holding a bit more quietly, but he felt just as relieved...and a lot more suspicious.

"Beth, I know you're aware that the action you took was a drastic one. You didn't come to California just to tell us that you want to date."

Beth's eyes shifted, and she pursed her lips. Lane's steady gaze made a slight chink in her breezy confidence, and she looked at her parents a little more warily.

Cynthia wondered if she should steel herself for something her imagination was too tired to even conceive.

Lane prompted Beth again. "Go on."

"Okay. Mom, Dad...I want us to spend the holidays together, and I'm not coming home unless you agree."

"What!"

"Where did that come from?" Cynthia stood up and realized that her hand was still in Lane's. He was staring at their daughter with a strange look in his narrowed eyes, and Cynthia had to tug three times before her hand came free.

"Beth," she said, taking two steps toward her daughter, "you brought us all the way here so you could issue ultimatums? Do you have any idea what could have happened to you alone at an airport in a city like Los Angeles? I imagined all sorts of things...."

She broke off when she realized that fatigue and fear were turning into anger, and, justified as she felt it would be, she didn't want to blow up here.

"Get whatever you brought, Beth. We're going back to Oregon and then we'll discuss this whole incident through. If you want to see your father more often, then we'll work something out. Of course, you'll be grounded for the next year, but maybe he can come—"

"I don't want to see him more often."

Cynthia turned to look at Lane, who had risen and was standing next to her now. He didn't bat an eye. "Thanks, pumpkin."

"I don't mean it that way. I mean that I didn't come here because I want to spend Christmas with you. I would have just asked if I wanted to do that. I want us to spend the holidays together, like a family. The *whole* holiday."

"Beth—" Cynthia began, the strain clear in her voice.

"Mom, I'm almost thirteen. I have never spent a holiday or a birthday with both my parents, and don't say that we did it when I was two, because that doesn't count. I'm sorry I worried you, but I had to make a statement, because otherwise you wouldn't have even considered it, and don't say you would have, because I asked you both last year and you both said no way."

"*I* don't remember being asked that," Lane muttered, looking at Cynthia accusingly.

"Yes, Dad," Beth insisted. "Last Easter I asked you if you thought it would be fun to spend a holiday with Mom, and you said to ask you again on April Fool's Day."

Cynthia eyed Lane disdainfully.

Beth put her hands on her hips. "And, Mom, you said that a holiday with Dad would be like—"

"Beth! I was speaking in general of the…stress holidays can add to relationships."

"You mean you weren't talking about Dad?"

Cynthia flicked a look in Lane's direction. "I would never speak disparagingly of your father in your presence, sweetheart."

Beth smiled and turned to walk around the couch. "So you would be willing for us all to spend time together, then?" She pinned her parents with a look of exquisite hopefulness.

Lane spoke first. "All right, Pancake."

Cynthia did a double take. They'd dubbed Beth "Pancake" when she was two months shy of her second birthday and had eaten three pancakes in one sitting. Cynthia still used the nickname herself.

Somehow she hadn't expected Lane to hang on to it.

Lane rested one hand on a hip still covered by rough denim jeans and raised the other hand to rub thoughtfully against the golden brown stubble that bearded his face.

"From now on, we'll try to work something out, to be together on your birthday, or—"

"No," Beth interrupted. "I want a whole holiday together. One whole holiday season that I can remember. Dad, you're not working on a script right now. And, Mom, you finished your book tour. Next year something else will come up or Mom will marry Alan or Dad will be with Vicki."

Neither Cynthia nor Lane would ever know the self-control it took each of them to keep from looking at the other when those names were mentioned. They had never heard specific names before, and they never, ever asked.

Cynthia pressed two fingers to her tired eyes. "Look, Beth, Pan—honey," she said, trying to understand her daughter's needs and avoid a migraine at the same time, "there aren't many *traditional* families around anymore, but that doesn't mean you don't have a family. You've got me and your father, and you have your grandparents and Aunt Gwen and her family." She took a step forward. "And, Pan— sweetie, we're going to have a wonderful holiday with Alan this year. The plans are all made, and you love San Juan Island."

"I spend my whole life on San Juan Island!" Beth exclaimed, throwing out her arms. "All I want is both of my parents in the same room at the same time."

"You can't force two people to spend time together and expect their lives to change, Bethie. This isn't a fairy tale."

"I don't want anybody's life to change," Beth answered quietly. "I just want some memories. You're *never* in the same room together. You don't even talk. Not even on my birthday. Someday I'll be married and have children and I'll want both of you to be there on special occasions. This would be good practice."

Once, when Cynthia and Lane were living in Oxnard, they had gone to the beach and a huge wave had barreled into them, hefting them as one body and spilling them out onto the shore. That was exactly how the guilt hit them now. But this time they didn't have each other's hands to hang on to.

Beth toyed with the end of her long braid, staring down at it. "I'm sorry I made you worry. I really am." She looked up again with the green eyes that always reminded Lane so much of Cynthia's. "I'm getting older, and everything's changing. We may not get another chance." She turned to the door. "I left my stuff in the living room. I'll go get it."

The parents watched their daughter leave the room. She was giving them time to talk.

Cynthia collapsed onto the couch. There wasn't enough time in the world to decide this and feel good about it. She didn't look at Lane. He backed up and sat down on the ottoman.

They both stayed silent, waiting for the other to speak first. Their thoughts were chugging along parallel tracks.

Beth wasn't a selfish or manipulative child, normally. There had been pain in her eyes, pleading in her voice, especially when she'd talked about them never being in the same room together.

The feeling of failure, dank and oppressive, settled on the room. Lane felt his chest growing numb even as his gut started to burn. It was an old feeling now, this sense of failure. Beth's words didn't inspire it—they just called it up again.

He saw family much the way his daughter did: two parents for every kid. No matter how fulfilling, how great single fatherhood could be, it was not the way he'd planned it. It was not at all the way he had imagined it would be thirteen years ago, when he'd walked into that little hospital in Virginia, carrying a dozen pink rosebuds and a pink bubble-gum cigar. Simple. But nothing had been simple after that.

His daughter wanted the temporary illusion of a traditional family. Not quite thirteen years old, and she was willing to settle for illusions.

Lane looked at Cynthia. What was she thinking? Her head was still bowed. He couldn't see her face, but he felt sure she was frowning. Was she wondering how to get out of this? Did she feel guilty at all, or had she weeded out that nasty emotion along with all the rest of them?

"Who's Alan?"

Cynthia raised her head. The question was abrupt, hard, and had a strange edge of suspicion. Lane's face looked like the question sounded.

She tensed. Automatically. And just as automatically assumed her "I-wrote-a-book-and-speak-to-groups" tone—professional, impermeable. "Alan is my male companion. Why?"

"I just want to know who you're planning to have

my daughter spend her Christmas vacation with.''
Lane answered equally coolly. '''Male companion.''' He rolled the title around on his tongue like
he was tasting a wine that had turned to vinegar. ''Is
that what they call it now up in Oregon?''

''Alan is a very good friend. He has a wonderful
home on San Juan Island. That's where we vacation,'' Cynthia informed him with infinite patience.
''Who's Vicki?''

Vicki was the friend with whom he shared holidays because they were both single, both without
family in California, and both tired of pretending
that turkey dinners in restaurants were as good as
turkey dinners at home. It was friendship, not a romance. But he wasn't going to tell Cynthia that. Not
now, not with Alan of San Juan Island thrown in his
face. Not when he felt like he'd just been told his
wife was cheating on him.

''Vicki,'' he said before he had time to think better of it, ''is my female *companion*,'' he replied,
drawing out the term with relish. ''She has a studio
apartment in North Hollywood, where we
get...companionable.''

Cynthia stood up in a furious rush, the blood
pounding in her ears drowning out all other sound.
''If that is an example of the prurient language and
behavior in which you indulge before my impres-
sionable, preteenage daughter, then I'm afraid the
judge will have to rethink visitation rights.'' She
tugged the sleeves down on her jacket and picked
her purse up off the couch.

Lane stood with her. ''Don't threaten me with
your two-bit morality speech! Just what do you do

with Beth when you and Alan are tucked up on the Island? Send her out to play in Puget Sound?"

"I have never acted in an unseemly fashion in front of my child—"

"Unseemly fashion? Oh, Miss Priss—"

"—and how dare you imply that I have? *How dare* you make fun of the way I speak?" she half gasped, half growled when she caught up with him.

"I wasn't implying anything. You said my behavior with Vicki was prurient."

"Because you were being deliberately crude, as per usual. And you took a potshot at my relationship with Alan."

"No, I—" Lane stopped himself. Yes, he had. He'd taken a potshot to start a fight with her. Again. "Yes, I did," he said aloud, shaking his head. He never fought anymore. Even in his screenplays, the good guys always got along.

"I'm sorry I called you Miss Priss." He looked in her eyes. They seemed a little liquidy. "I didn't really hurt your feelings, did I, Cyn?" He took a step forward.

She turned to look for the purse she'd flung a few potshots back.

"Pfff." She dismissed the idea while she searched the sofa cushions. The last time she raised her voice like that, it was 1983. This was not the way she conducted herself anymore. She mumbled the only concession she could think of. "You're not really crude."

Lane grinned, plucked her purse off the floor and held it out to her. "Yes, I am," he said agreeably. "But never around Beth."

Cynthia accepted the clutch bag and nodded.

"Well, at this rate, we'll be on 'Sally Jessy Raphael' by morning."

"Arguing on national television? I can't afford the publicity."

"Neither can I."

"That's right," Lane agreed, sitting on the couch. This time Cynthia took the ottoman. "You've got that group. Romance…what is it?"

"Romantics Anonymous. It's a modified twelve-step program."

"For compulsive romantics?" he queried politely.

"*Ex*-compulsive romantics," she answered, smiling.

"Ahh." He nodded, then frowned. "But in twelve-step programs, aren't you supposed to consider yourself always in the process of recovering, rather than completely cured?"

Feigned ignorance, she longed to inform him, had a stench that was stronger than trout wrapped in gym socks.

Instead, Cynthia smiled more patiently. "Each anonymous group is unique, and each member has his or her own definitions. Personally, I considered myself cured when I developed a new way of thinking that would make it impossible to return to an old bad habit."

Lane's brows rose and stayed there. *Nice one,* he acknowledged. So he was an old bad habit, huh?

He leaned forward on his arms, with his elbows on his thighs. "Still," he persisted, his tone curious and laced with friendly concern, "it probably wouldn't be a good idea for someone to be around an old bad habit for a long period of time—say, a whole school vacation. My friend Lester Willis stayed clear of alcohol for six years after he sobered up. Restaurants, markets, parties…you name it. If there was liquor present, Les stayed away…because the temptation was always there.''

"The implication being—'' Cynthia smiled, stretching politeness to its absolute limit ''—that *I* am the alcoholic and *you* are the bottle?''

Lane smiled and leaned back, crossing his legs. "No, no, no, I only mean… Well, yeah.''

"You—'' Cynthia rose, an amazed laugh trapped in her throat ''—are unbelievable. You honestly believe that's an accurate appraisal?''

"I think I cut pretty close to the bone, yeah.''

She looked at him, disbelief at his arrogance written on her face. "Then you're a ninny.'' Grasping her purse so tightly that her knuckles turned white, she put one fist on her hip. "If there was an Idiots Anonymous, you'd need a tutor to get in.''

Lane stood, his own hands going to his hips as he leaned forward. "Don't call me a ninny, Cynthia.''

There was barely a foot between them already, and Cynthia took a step closer. She glared in his face and opened her mouth to take the bait, then came to her senses and shook her head. "I do not do this anymore,'' she muttered to herself, taking several steps away from Lane.

Dang it, what was she doing? Her life now was a paean to sanity, a living testimony to the fact that serenity blossomed in a garden watered with reason and calm. She took a long, cleansing breath and began again.

"We need to think about Beth and this holiday she wants, not our innumerable differences.''

Lane rubbed his forehead and nodded, the wind out of his sails. "You're right. We have to get through this holiday without strife. That is, if we're going to do it." He looked at Cynthia, who wavered uncertainly.

"I'm not a hundred percent sure we should give in to this," she said.

"I understand. If you don't think you can do it, we should decide that now before Beth comes back."

"*I* can do it," Cynthia said calmly. "I've had training, after all, in reacting from a sane and logical center. All I need is a little rest to keep my balance."

"That's right, you don't believe in letting emotion run away with you anymore." Lane nodded. "I have to admit, I still react from my gut first. It wouldn't be good for Beth to see us fighting all through Christmas." He looked at her and lifted a brow. "Kind of hard for two people who were once married to be detached, though, isn't it?"

"Not at all." Cynthia shook her head emphatically. "In fact, I'm glad you used that word. *Detached* is exactly what we'll need to be in order to get through this holiday. At all times we must be able to access our ability to reason through our feelings and to act on them wisely."

Lane glanced at her feet to see if she was standing on a soapbox. "We were never very detached in our marriage."

"Exactly," Cynthia agreed carefully. "We didn't have clarity."

"Clarity," Lane mused. "So that's what you mean in your book. I saw the 'Jack Phelpps Show,'" he said when Cynthia looked at him in surprise. "You think that the more valid relationships are the ones with clarity...with a certain detachment, is that right?"

"They're certainly more sane."

"Probably, but are they as much fun?"

Cynthia laughed and raised her chin confidently. "Absolutely."

Lane nodded slowly. "Well, I have to hand it to you. And to Alan. Detachment is not something I've coveted in a relationship. Then again, when I think of all the times you and I let passion dictate our behavior..." He let the sentence trail off and shook his head, a slow, lazy smile telling her, *I'm thinking of a few of those times right now.* "That weekend in Gold Beach when we were supposed to be cramming. The Rhododendron Dell in Golden Gate Park." His eyes widened a moment and then he frowned abruptly before saying, "That stable in Santa Fe. All that fresh hay... Nope, you're right. We were crazy. I'm sure that what you and Alan have going is a lot more sane."

Lane shoved his hands in his pockets and smiled at her guilelessly. "You know, I haven't had the courage to try marriage again. Haven't wanted to chance another divorce. But maybe you and Alan will change my mind. Maybe you can show me how much more rewarding a calm, detached, logical relationship can be."

Lane nodded thoughtfully and walked to the door. "I'm going to see what's keeping Beth. I'll tell her we've decided to go ahead with the family holiday. Right, Cyn?"

"Right."

Lane peered at her. "Do you know your lips

didn't even move when you said that? Neat trick.''
His expression was contemplative, almost placid, yet
Cynthia couldn't fail to notice the challenging glint
in his dark eyes. She had a sinking feeling in her
stomach when he spoke. ''I don't mind telling you,
Cynthia,'' he said quietly, ''I'm looking forward to
this month. I think it could be a real learning experience. For all of us.''

Chapter Four

Cynthia sighed and felt tingling warmth flow through her limbs, melting away the tightness and the fatigue. Relaxation, that's what it was. She was finally relaxed.

She was also asleep. Being asleep was the *only* way she could have felt relaxed lying in her ex-husband's bed.

She stretched her arms over her head, her legs toward the foot of the bed, and twisted her body on the down-filled comforter. She came to rest in an incomparably comfortable position—on her side with her arms tucked under her head, one leg straight out and the other knee drawn up.

As she swam up through sleep and into consciousness, thoughts started flitting in and out of her mind.

Where is Beth?

How long have I been sleeping?

Is that sunlight coming through the blinds or is it the light from a street lamp?

I'm hungry.

Lane has a king-size bed.

Her eyelids clicked open as if somebody had just pressed a control switch. She grieved briefly for the lovely, soft, sleepy feeling that was fading even as tension wormed its insidious way back into her stomach.

She and Lane hadn't spoken to each other at all on the interminable ride back from Gwen's house. Fortunately, Beth had filled all the silent spaces and then some. She had bubbled over with anticipation in the car, her words spilling and somersaulting joyously as she listed a veritable cornucopia of family activities she wanted them to try.

Cynthia sighed and rolled onto her back again. The bedroom door clicked open. She stayed still and quiet until she heard a soft voice whisper to her.

"Mom?"

"Bethie. I overslept." She smiled and stretched a hand out toward her daughter.

Beth bounced onto the mattress and settled near Cynthia's waist. "That's okay. You're sleep-deprived. That's what Dad said."

"Oh, is that what I am?" Cynthia smoothed her fingers across the braid that hung over Beth's shoulder.

"Do you smell the soup? Dad's cooking—"

"Bethie!" The reverberating whisper came from the hallway. "Beth!"

Beth hopped off the bed and ran over to the door. "I'm here, Dad," she rasped back.

"Hey, I told you to let your mother sleep. She needs—"

"She's awake," Beth whispered again, then giggled as Lane came to the bedroom door. "She's going to be hungry. She's always hungry when she gets up."

Lane looked into the room as the doorbell rang. "I remember," he said quietly, his gaze on Cynthia.

Beth squeezed past her father and out of the room. "I'll get the door."

"Look through the peephole!"

"Ask who it is!"

Lane and Cynthia called after her at the same time.

Lane looked back into the room to see Cynthia struggling to rise up on an elbow.

"*Are* you hungry?" He stood with one hand on the doorknob. There was a dish towel in the other hand. "I've got soup going. Mulligatawny."

Cynthia swung her legs over the edge of his bed and reached delicately under one thigh, wiggling a little in the hopes of unobtrusively pulling her skirt down. She raised a hand to her hair, which was in more disarray than ever after her nap. Her voice and her eyes were still heavy with fatigue.

"Campbell's makes Mulligatawny now?"

Lane laughed because there was nothing snide about the question; she was too sleepy to know how rude it sounded. "I don't know about Campbell's," he said, grinning, "but *I* make it pretty well."

He leaned against the doorframe and folded his arms. It was quite a show, watching Cynthia struggle to get her bearings and compose herself while her slim, stockinged feet felt around on the floor for her shoes. Only Cynthia could make the attempt at covering awkwardness seem at once clumsy and sexy.

Hearing voices in his living room, he reluctantly pushed away from the wall. "Dinner will be ready when you are. We'll be in the kitchen."

Cynthia watched him leave. She stood, tugging at her skirt, which was hopelessly twisted around her legs, and walked into the master bathroom. One flick of a switch and the room filled with lights, warm overhead lights, soft lights pouring in from the sides of the long mirror above the sink, and muted lights glowing from behind a frosted strip that ran along the base of the mirror.

Cynthia peered into the mirror and gasped. How wonderful to be able to see herself at this moment with such startling clarity. Her head looked like the Scarecrow's in *The Wizard of Oz*—straw-colored hair was sticking out everywhere. Her eyes were puffy, her cheeks were puffy, her lips were puffy. Why was it that at age twenty you could wake up from a nap looking like you'd just been kissed, and at thirty-four you woke up looking like you were retaining water?

"You look fine," she told her image loyally. "You look…good. For a thirty-four-year-old single parent who's been out of her mind with worry and wearing the same clothes for two days, you look…almost human."

She rested her elbows on the sink—charcoal granite—and plopped her head heavily onto her hands. She felt like crying and she didn't know why.

Her whole life was about to be turned upside down and she couldn't even go into it with a decent hairdo. She raised her head and stared into the glass.

She led workshops; she'd written a book. She was a strong woman, and she had three good answers for every question.

So why was it that Lane Lincoln could turn her into a human nerve ending who had three anxious questions for every answer?

Please, God, don't let me be a marshmallow.

So what if Lane's sheets felt like silk? So what if *she* slept on polyester-blend bed linen that felt as sensuous as cardboard? So what if she hadn't been able to swallow when Lane walked into the bedroom?

Hearing a clock chime in the hallway, Cynthia listened for the bells. She counted six. She and Beth were scheduled to fly back to Oregon at 10:00 p.m. They would have about two hours in Lane's company before they had to leave for the airport.

Two hours. In the early days of their relationship, two hours together had been far too little; two hours apart had been torture. Now it was completely the reverse.

Moving quickly, Cynthia splashed water on her face and stuffed her hair one more time into her lumpy chignon. She scooted to the bed and stuffed her feet into the pumps that were, as always, dyed to match her suit. The image consultant her publicist had hired said that matching shoes were a ''power look.''

Moving out of the bedroom and through the hall, she headed toward the sound of voices. She entered the living room, noticing for the first time the ceramic Mickey Mouse clock and a framed print depicting King Arthur and Guinevere.

Cynthia stared at the print a moment. Her sister's

given name was Guinevere. Their father had insisted on a romantic name for his second-born daughter after reluctantly agreeing to the more prosaic Cynthia for his eldest. Her father would have loved the clock and the print. Like Lane, he had revered anything romantic or whimsical. And, like Lane, he had found the responsibilities of family and day-to-day life too mundane and restricting to tolerate for long.

Laughter came from the kitchen. It was soft, cozy laughter. Cynthia followed the sound, expecting to find Lane and Beth. The sight which greeted her was a surprise. Lane stood next to the sink, his tall form protected by a red apron that bore in black the command "Love me, love my cooking." He had a knife in one hand, a tomato in the other, and a smile on his face. Beth was standing to his left, holding three lemons, which she'd apparently been attempting to juggle. The surprise was seated at the square oak table in the middle of the room. She was slicing into a huge, round shepherd's bread.

The woman's face was open, warm and expressive. Her skin was golden, even though it was winter; her blue eyes were bright and candid. Her deep brown hair was thick, curly and cut in a very contemporary bob. And her shoes were off; her bare feet rested on Lane's Spanish tile.

For a moment no one said anything. Hands stopped moving, knives stopped slicing midmotion as though someone had hollered, "Freeze!"

Lane spoke first. "Hello, Cyn," he said and then quickly added, "-thia," as though the abbreviated name was too informal or too personal in front of his guest. "Welcome back to the living. You look more rested."

"Thanks." Cynthia nodded at the supposed compliment.

Lane smiled a little to hide his sudden discomfort. She didn't really look more rested, but she did look adorable. Her sleek, classic hairstyle had turned into a wispy, haphazard arrangement—one that sorely tempted him to reach out, and with the gentlest touch, send her blond hair tumbling loose around her shoulders. She was wearing her high heels, but her panty hose were bagging around her left knee, and he knew for a fact that there was a thin run riding up the other leg from her heel to...well, as far as he'd been able to see when she'd lain on her side on his bed, with one leg bent, the other extended, and her skirt twisted around her slender thighs.

He swallowed hard. The scene could have been so natural, with his wife ambling into the kitchen from an after-work nap to find her husband and daughter preparing her dinner. The husband would walk over to the sleepy wife, kiss her solidly in full view of the daughter, who would giggle, and the mother and father would advance on the child, prepared to tickle her into respect.

Lane's fingers tightened around the tomato he was holding. Yeah, it could have been like that, but in his kitchen there was only tension, and for Beth's sake he sought to diffuse it.

"Sit down, Cynthia." He pointed the paring knife toward a chair.

Cynthia smiled at Beth, who was smelling one of the lemons and glancing between her mother and the woman already seated at the table.

Cynthia moved to the table and sat, smiling politely at the brunette, who extended her arm above the bread.

"I'm Vicki. I'm a friend of Lane's. Beth tells me you've been traveling a great deal." Vicki looked at Cynthia with genuine interest.

She was likable, Cynthia thought. Friendly and unguarded, with an ingenuous expression in her blue eyes. She was older than Cynthia had first imagined when Lane had mentioned the studio apartment in North Hollywood and their…activity there. Vicki had pretty laugh lines around her expressive eyes. She was full and womanly. She was earth, and at the moment Cynthia felt like air. She nodded at Vicki.

"Yes. I didn't really have enough time to sight-see, but I did manage to get to Vermont." She threw a slanting look at her daughter. "I brought Beth some maple candy. It's in my purse."

Without asking either parent for permission to indulge in straight sugar before dinner, Beth let out a whoop and exclaimed, "I'm gettin' it!"

She ran from the kitchen toward Lane's bedroom, where Cynthia had left her purse.

Lane shook his head and started to slice the tomato. "So, you made it to Vermont," he commented casually. Cynthia had wanted to see Vermont when they were married, but somehow they'd never made it. "And were the trees as spectacular as you thought they'd be?"

"Yes." Cynthia cleared her throat a little and rubbed a finger over a spot on the table top. "Yes, they were."

Lane was standing at an angle to the counter as he prepared the salad. He glanced up briefly at

Vicki. "Cynthia has a thing for trees. She thinks they have personalities." He smiled and looked at his ex-wife. "What was it you called that willow tree in your mother's yard? 'It'?"

"*Cousin* It," Cynthia admitted tightly. She did not want to look like a nitwit in front of an attractive, comfortably barefoot woman whose hair was brushed.

"That's right, Cousin It from 'The Addams Family.'" His smile turned into a full-fledged grin. "You should have seen it, Vick. The leaves hung down to the ground. All you could see was the base of the trunk. Cynthia thought it might be lonely because it looked so different from the other trees, and she'd go into the yard and have a conversation with it every time she visited her mother."

He turned his gaze back to Cynthia and asked, his voice low, "How is Cousin It?"

Cynthia knew that her mouth was open and that she was staring, but she was having a hard time rectifying either condition. How did he know that she'd talked to the tree? She'd never told anyone, and she'd asked Cousin It not to say anything— Her mouth slammed shut.

"It got beetle rot," she snapped matter-of-factly in answer to Lane's question. "We pulled it up."

Lane paused in the middle of shredding a carrot. "That's too bad," he said, and he truly meant it.

He'd loved the whimsical side of Cynthia's nature, a side she'd exposed all too infrequently. He'd only found out about her lengthy conversations with Cousin It because he'd sneaked into the yard one night to scare her and heard her having a heart-to-heart with the tree. He'd fallen more in love with her in that moment, and he'd hoped that her fanciful side would blossom the longer they were together, the more she trusted that he would cherish and respect her secret fancies as much as she did. But it hadn't worked out that way.

And now, he thought as his eyes absorbed her schoolmarm posture and the unyielding set of her lips, now she was straighter than a dead horse's tail.

Beth came back into the kitchen, a hunk of maple candy hanging out of her mouth and the box clutched in her hands.

"This is s-o-o-o good!" She swooned, holding the box out. "Anybody want some?"

"I'll try some," Vicki said gamely when it looked like the other adults weren't going to answer at all.

Beth came over to the kitchen table, sitting on her knees on the chair. "I can't wait to travel east. I want to see Vermont and New York and Virginia. I was born in Virginia."

"You were?" Vicki said, giving the candy a lick. "I didn't know that. I assumed you were born in Oregon."

"Nope." Beth leaned her elbows on the table and proceeded to deliver information as though only she and Vicki were in the room. "My parents traveled a lot back then. They had this old trailer, and they hooked it up to a truck and moved around like vagabonds."

Lane's gaze snapped to Cynthia.

"I was born in Virginia," Beth continued, "but I've never been back. Mom doesn't like to travel much."

"I didn't know your father did, either," Vicki

said, shifting in her chair to look at Lane. She laughed and shook her head. "Is that why you're such a homebody now, because you traveled so much in your youth?"

Cynthia's mouth puckered more at that news. She'd begged him to settle down, to pick one place—any place—and to stay there, so they could begin to put down roots and feel like a real family. It had meant the world to her back then. But he'd needed the inspiration of different towns, different people, to complete the screenplay he had steadfastly believed would be their big start. And then he'd left her in Oregon to put down roots without him while he traipsed off with a dream and a prayer to Hollywood.

Lane wiped his hands on a dish towel and lifted a pot lid to check the soup. "A lot of things I did when I was younger don't seem as appealing now," he said simply. "We'd better get hopping if we're going to get to the airport on time."

Cynthia watched her daughter and the two other adults move through the kitchen like a well-choreographed dance company as they finished the preparations for dinner.

Beth crossed left to get the glasses. Vicki crossed right and reached for the bread plates. Lane countered Vicki and picked up a salad bowl. Vicki brushed past Lane to serve the soup.

No one had to instruct or ask for anything. They worked as a unit. At one point as Lane was crossing behind Vicki, he reached over and patted her rear. Vicki's startled gaze swung from Lane to Cynthia and then back to the stick of butter she was unwrapping. Fortunately Beth had her head in the refrigerator. Cynthia quickly glanced away to study the track lighting.

Dinner moved swiftly with Beth once again providing most of the conversation, informing Cynthia that Vicki was an actress and informing Vicki that Cynthia was—probably—the best mother in the universe.

Vicki came along for the ride to the airport. She insisted that they stay till the plane took off, but Cynthia insisted just as strongly that Lane and Vicki should get back on the road. They had a long drive ahead of them, and Beth was already falling asleep in the waiting area. She'd been awake since before dawn.

Lane kissed his daughter, promised he would see her in Oregon in a week and nodded a goodbye to Cynthia. "Have a safe flight."

"We will. I'll call in a couple of days to firm things up."

Lane nodded again and escorted Vicki in silence back to the car.

No one had eaten much dinner, so Lane pulled up to a fast-food burger place on the way home. They decided to eat in the parking lot, in his car.

Lane was squeezing ranch dressing onto his fries when he and Vicki both decided to break their tense silence.

"Vicki, I can't tell you how sorry—"

"Lane, you're a jerk."

They looked at each other and spoke again.

"I know."

"You should be sorry."

Then they stared out the windshield a moment.

Lane shook his head. He knew he had to finish his apology, but this wasn't going to come easily.

"I'm sorry I patted your..."

"Butt," Vicki said succinctly. "You touched my butt. You know," she said, biting down hard on a fry, "it's not that I would mind your doing that under different circumstances, it's just the reason you did it that bothers me. I don't appreciate being used to make other people jealous. It's a betrayal of our friendship."

She dropped the rest of her fry into the bag and spoke more quietly. "That *is* what you were doing, isn't it? Trying to make Cynthia jealous?"

Lane kept looking straight out the windshield. "Yes."

Vicki sighed. "So much for my goddesslike patience. I know you never offered anything other than friendship, but since you never date anyone else, either, I thought—" She cut herself off and looked down at her sandwich. "Why do I always get the fish?" she mumbled. "Let me have a bite of your burger."

Lane handed it over, his expression candidly showing his surprise. Vicki grabbed the burger, took a huge bite and handed it back as she said with her mouth stuffed, "So, tell me about your wife."

Lane ignored that question for the moment and said gently, "Vicki, if I'd had any idea that you...I would have..."

"Oh, shut up." Vicki swallowed her burger as Lane trailed off. "Don't you know anything about confession etiquette? You're supposed to slide over my little disclosure with a very flattered look and maybe a quick caress of my tender cheek—but not with greasy fingers, please.'' She pointed a warning finger at him.

Lane laughed and privately vowed eternal gratitude to this woman for easing them both over a rough spot.

He held up both hands and waggled his fingers. ''Haven't touched a fry yet.''

Vicki rolled her eyes reluctantly. ''Oh, all right, but make it quick and painless—I want another bite of your burger.''

Lane cupped Vicki's cheek with his palm, rubbing his thumb once across the smooth skin. She grinned and said, ''That's enough. Tell me about your wife.''

Lane switched sandwiches with her. ''I'm not sure what to say.''

''Tell me what broke you up. You always made it sound like she just decided one day that she didn't want to be married anymore. Like that character in the movie we saw last week? 'Thanks for the marriage, but I really hate men.' But it isn't like that at all, is it?''

''No. I think she may have hated *me* for a while, but I don't think she hates men.'' He turned to his friend. ''How did you glean all of this? Cynthia barely spoke tonight.''

''Oh, she spoke, all right. She may not have said much, but she couldn't take her eyes off you. Except when she was eyeballing me.'' She took in Lane's expression of wonder and reached for her soda. ''Men are so dumb.'' She spent several quiet moments sipping her drink through a straw.

''All right,'' she said, her voice offering compassion and at the same time warning of an absolute impatience with nonsense, "so why did you break up? Why do you think she hated you?"

Lane hooked a wrist over the steering wheel. "She wanted more from our marriage." His eyes narrowed. "I was traveling a lot then, writing articles on small-town life for a magazine in Oregon. And I was working on my first screenplay. It wasn't easy—there wasn't much money." He grimaced. "There wasn't *any* money. Cynthia and I got odd jobs here and there, but we were living day to day."

Lane threw out a hand and just missed knocking Vicki's soda over. "I liked our life. I thought she did, too. It was just the two of us—we were out on the road seeing places we'd never seen before. We were young…we had plenty of time to settle down. I don't think she ever believed I'd make a living as a screenwriter. Or she didn't want to wait."

He stared down at his food, then out the window, every bit of his concentration focused on looking back now, on making sense of the past. Vicki could tell that he'd traveled this road before, but had never reached a destination. She saw confusion on his face, and, the more he talked, she saw pain.

"I wanted to marry Cynthia more than I'd ever wanted anything in my life. After Beth came, we moved back to Oregon and her stepfather gave me a job in his appliance store."

Lane wagged his head and laughed without a trace of humor. "I hated it, Vick. I was suffocating there. A friend of mine from college called and told me about a job where he was working…nothing much, but I'd be closer to the studios. I moved to L.A. and Cynthia stayed in Oregon. I thought it would be for a few months at the most. Just till I got somebody to look at my script and got settled enough for her and Beth to come out, but..."

He shrugged and glanced at Vicki sardonically. "Hollywood's a slow town when you don't know anybody. And then some nitwit little delivery person came into where I worked, tossed divorce papers at me and said, 'Sorry, buddy.' I almost hit him."

Vicki nodded slowly. "Were you scared?"

"I was pissed!"

"Yeah, but were you scared, too?"

Lane rubbed a hand over his face. "Vicki, you ask a lot of questions."

"A lot of *pertinent* questions." She didn't need his answer to know that it was true—he had been scared. Petrified, unless she missed her guess.

Vicki was very aware that Lane had lost his family—mother, father and older sister—in a car crash when he was eight years old. She'd lost her own family to a variety of illnesses, and she knew how guilty and how alone she'd often felt as the only one left alive. She understood the terror, as well—the fear every time she got close to someone that she'd do something to make *them* disappear, too.

"Okay," she said. "So you were scared and you never told her. And you were really ticked that she was going to leave you willingly, the way we thought our families did— Wow, this is great stuff for the couch."

Lane tried to smile. He knew Vicki wasn't being irreverent, but he couldn't stop blaming Cynthia for not believing in him, for never coming back to him, for closing the door with her rapid divorce proceedings...and for writing a book and living a life that disavowed everything they'd had together—the romance, the passion, and yes, the sex. She'd turned her back on it and, as far as he could tell, hadn't missed it.

Vicki's soft voice broke through the anger he was building in his mind.

"Why haven't you told her that you still love her?"

"It's not that simple—" Lane began to answer immediately, anger and resentment lacing his tone. Then he stopped, the tension draining just a bit from his stiff body. "Maybe she's right, Vicki. Maybe this... feeling I get when I look at her, maybe it isn't enough. It wasn't enough the first time."

"Have you ever gotten that feeling with anybody else?"

"No."

"Ever come close?"

Lane shook his head.

"Ever experienced a feeling that could be a good substitute?"

"No," Lane said quietly. "I haven't."

Vicki sighed and looked out at the parking lot.

"True love is just like chocolate," she said philosophically. "I ate a whole bag of carob malt balls once. Went right back out and bought a chocolate bar that could've choked a horse. Once you've had the real thing, there's no turning back." She tossed her napkins and the rest of her food into the bag they'd saved for trash. "Of course, I have read that people who are sex-starved eat enormous amounts of chocolate as a temporary substitute."

She reached over to Lane and gathered his un-eaten food, as well. "I think you've got one good fight left in you, old man. Give it your best shot."

Lane said nothing for a moment. Then he spoke. "Vicki. Have I ever told you that I love you?"

His eyes were warm and sincere. His voice was soft and gentle. Vicki shook her head and smiled.

Lane started the car, and Vicki leaned back in her bucket seat. As they pulled out of the parking lot, she said, "Oh, did I tell you what Cynthia bought to take on the plane while you were checking the gate number?"

Lane frowned and shook his head.

"A king-size chocolate bar, a box of brownies, and a pound of fudge."

The house seemed oppressively quiet when Lane returned. He wandered from room to room, straightening up. Cynthia was everywhere, perched on a stool in the kitchen, even curled up in his bed. His mind was filled with her image—the sound of her voice, her laughter, the way she leaned her head to one side when she was listening, the way she crossed her legs when she was nervous.

His heart-to-heart chat with Vicki hadn't helped. For so long the past had been like a picture he'd bravely fought to keep fuzzy and out of focus. Now, against his will, the focus was painfully clear.

He remembered the day, the hour, the very moment he'd found her. A bright September afternoon in 1977, Room 203, Gilbert Hall on the University of Oregon campus in Eugene. It was the first meeting of a course in nineteenth-century American poetry. Lane had signed up seeking inspiration.

He knew at once that he'd found it.

Cynthia Erin James sat directly across from him, with her books on the floor by her feet, a clipboard with lined paper positioned unobtrusively on the brown table the students shared, and her hands resting neatly on her lap when she wasn't writing. She didn't spread herself out like the other students did. She didn't raise her hand to add her two cents to every exploration of a poem. She did sit enraptured, devouring every discussion, and it amazed Lane that each time her shy gaze lifted, she seemed to be listening with her eyes.

She had green eyes. And when she looked up, Lane stopped caring about metaphors and similes. All he wanted to know was how to talk to the girl with eyes like wishing wells.

Twice he tried to speak to her after class, but she eluded him both times. If he tried to catch her eye, she invariably glanced away. He never stepped in where he wasn't invited, but this was different. She needed him.

And then they wrote poems. Reading the poems aloud to the class was optional; Lane read his.

''Grant me one gift, my love, my soul:
That I may enter the chamber where your heart dwells
And spend my days plucking books from your shelves.
Would I learn from those tomes the secrets in your eyes?
Eyes green as the ocean, skin pale as a moon, hair kissed by the starlight and warmed by the sun—this is my love.
Each day that I see her, I yearn a bit more.
Brown Formica and shyness are what keep us apart,

But nothing will keep me away from her heart...."

The poem raged on, but the class was out of control. They were giggling and oohing long before he reached the final rhyming couplet.

Even Dr. Percy Anderson, who really only appreciated Milton, smiled and glanced at Cynthia as he jotted a very generous C- into his gradebook.

Lane lifted his head from the paper and grinned at his girl—at least, he felt certain that, barring an arranged marriage or novitiate vows, she soon would be his girl.

His brown eyes rose to meet her "ocean greens." She met his look directly, and she didn't look shy now. Her luscious lips were slightly parted; her adorable nose and cheeks were red.

Lane stopped smiling.

She was embarrassed—and madder than a dog with his nose full of cat claws. She grabbed her books and her clipboard and ran from the class, and Lane knew a sorrow that socked him in the gut and made his heart feel hollow. He felt like he'd just shot a deer.

He had the presence of mind to murmur "Excuse me" to the stunned professor and curious class, but he left his poem and his books behind as he followed her.

His one thought as he jogged down the corridor was that she must be used to running away because she moved pretty damned quickly.

"Wait!" he called to her as he reached the glass

doors of the building. "Will you wait a minute… please!"

He didn't bother to modulate his powerful baritone, and a handful of people in a classics discussion session leaned their chairs back to see who was running through the hallway.

She didn't even spare him a glance.

He caught up with her outside the building, near some trees, but only after he barely missed knocking a comparative lit professor's coffee and doughnuts all the way to the social ecology lab.

"Look, the least you could do is stop long enough to tell me to go to hell. Dr. Reed almost sacrificed his crullers so I could apologize to you."

She stopped by a tree, but didn't turn around.

He jogged up, then circled around her so he could see her face. He let the need to slow his breathing buy him a little time.

God, she was beautiful.

Not like a model. Not like the campus cheerleaders or like the sorority girls he met at parties. Her skin was free of makeup, her expression devoid of artifice.

Her glossy hair was pulled back into the simplest of ponytails. It hung, silky and thick and straight, to accentuate a neck as slender and fine as a flower stalk. He could see the pulse under her jaw and the almost contradictory strength of her collarbone. Never before had he realized that a neck could speak volumes.

He completely forgot that he was going to apologize.

His eyes roamed at will and his words glided out on a whisper, like a prayer. ''You are beautiful.''

When Cynthia looked at him, tears hovered in her beguiling eyes. She dropped her books, heedless of where they fell, and raised her arms. Mesmerized, Lane slowly opened for her embrace. Cynthia placed her palms on his chest, leaned back just a bit and then shoved with all her muscle.

Caught off guard and off balance, Lane fell right on his butt.

Stunned, he wasn't immediately capable of doing anything more than staring up at her, but when she bent to collect her textbooks, her chest heaving with her breath, his hand shot out like a cornered snake to close around her wrist.

''A little verbal elaboration could go a long way here,'' he told her, wishing she would raise her head. ''Look, I'm sorry if I embarrassed you, but, frankly, you don't seem too shy right now. I mean, what the hell did I do? I read a poem that was pretty damn flattering, if you ask me. If you think about it, I'm the one who was really vulnerable in there. I'm the one who took the risk.''

Lane frowned slightly as the words left his mouth. Okay, so as an apology it could use a little polish, but it was, at least in part, true.

Cynthia was looking at him now, her eyes wide and angry and disbelieving.

''Let go of my wrist.''

That was all she intended to say. Lane could hear it in the low, calm finality of her tone.

''You're going to run away again, aren't you?'' he asked softly. ''This'll be the third time. You've run away from me twice so far and we haven't even gotten to midterm.'' He let go of her wrist. ''Why?''

She gathered her books and stood, but didn't move. Lane stood with her. She was tall, he realized for the first time, five foot six or seven to his six feet. She folded both arms around her books and held them to her chest while she watched him warily.

''I don't know what you mean.''

''Why did the poem bother you so much?''

Again her eyes widened in disbelief. ''You played your joke at my expense.''

Her voice was mellow, low, he thought, even now when her eyes were flashing. It was a woman's voice. He struggled not to lose himself in the feel of it. He needed to hear her words.

''I really wanted to take that class,'' Cynthia said, her gaze focusing on the building behind him. ''Now I have to sit there with everybody knowing I was the butt of your fraternity humor.''

She turned to face him directly. It surprised Lane.

''Taking that class wasn't easy for me. I have a hard time speaking in groups like that. This may be hard for a dumb jock like you to understand, but after your little joke, it's going to be almost impossible for me.''

Lane's frown lowered a little more with every point she made. Finally, he shook his head and decided to tackle the most important one. ''I was not playing a joke on you. I was not making fun of you.''

He paused a moment, not sure how to tell her the next in a way that would make her believe it. Surprising himself, he actually felt a little sheepish.

"I was trying," he said, his lips lifting in a self-mocking grin, "to sweep you off your feet. I've been trying for the past three weeks, but you keep running away."

He saw the surprise, the shock register. He saw the doubt and the confusion that swiftly replaced it, and he saw her struggle to make her face a neutral mask. She could not, however—and he was glad to see it—tamper with the feeling in those heartbreaking green eyes. They were wide beneath her silky frown as she addressed herself to the least disturbing comment he made.

"I still don't know what you mean about running away."

He smiled softly. "Every time I try to talk to you."

"When?" Her voice dropped to a mumble. "I'm sorry. I didn't know you were trying to talk to me."

"I followed you from class twice," he began in disbelief, then remembered that there were other people around both times. She was too shy to assume that a stranger wanted to talk to her. He wondered what had made her that way and for a moment wanted to ask, but then a peace, a comfort, settled over him like a balm. He wouldn't need to learn everything all at once. Somehow, Lane knew he would have the time.

Oregon rain, reliable and tranquilizing as an old friend, drizzled down on them in large, gentle drops.

"You're an English major," Lane stated, looking at the books in her arms. "Do you want to teach?"

"No...write," she said softly, like she'd never dared to say the words before.

"Me too," Lane said just as softly, even though he said the words often, to anyone who would listen.

The rain beat a bit harder. Lane was wearing a nylon jacket. Cynthia was wearing a cotton shirt, short-sleeved and thin.

Without asking, Lane peeled off his jacket, then reached around and over her head to wrap it around her shoulders. No "May I" was ventured, no "Thank you" returned. Neither was really needed.

It felt good for him to give.

It felt good for her to take.

Chapter Five

Lane rose from the ocean looking like a Greek god on steroids.

His brown hair hung in a thick wet tail down his neck. Water streamed from his hairline, down his face and off his chin; it glistened on his shoulders and ran in rivulets down his chest and over the hard, rippling muscles of his stomach.

Cynthia didn't even bother to try to keep her gaze above his navel—not when so much was going on below it. His trunks were purple, a deep purple that made him look like he'd risen mysteriously from the undersea world to walk on land. And his steps were bringing him right toward her.

His expression was intent—as though he had a specific purpose in walking toward her—and despite her desire to remain cool, unruffled, sophisticated, Cynthia's stomach fluttered beneath her sedate maillot. Despite her desire to stay in control, her legs started to feel like they were filled with jelly when he dropped to the blanket she was lying on. And her shallow breathing belied the indifference she would have pretended. He trailed his fingers along her collarbone, and she felt pleasure warming her skin like sunshine. She closed her eyes and smiled as the straps of her maillot were rolled off her shoulders and down her arms....

"Stop, stop, stop! Just stop it!"

Cynthia was holding a potato in one hand and a potato peeler in the other. She slapped both onto the kitchen counter as she grit her teeth and leaned over the sink. It had been one week since she'd seen Lane, and she hadn't stopped thinking about him—remembering him—since.

The memories hit at any time, any place, regardless of what innocuous task she'd assigned herself to keep occupied. Yesterday she'd been bleaching mildew off the bathroom tile when she'd recalled the Japanese standing bath they'd tried in Longhollow, Wisconsin.

She'd dealt with this problem before, of course, with people in her R.A. meetings. She was in relapse. She was remembering the romance and forgetting the pain.

Think pain, she reminded herself, picking up the potato and peeler again. *Think emotional agony.*

It would have been a simple thing if not for the fact that the object of her wayward thoughts was getting into town tonight. He was going to check into a motel and meet everyone for dinner at Cynthia's mother's house. The whole family would be there, including Gwen, Franklin and their children, who were spending the entire month of December in Oregon. Cynthia was making potato salad—

Lane's *least* favorite side dish. If he said anything, she'd just look confused and say she didn't remember his likes and dislikes. It would be some small satisfaction after the last week of picturing him as he'd been…and then picturing him with Vicki.

The doorbell rang. It had to be Gwen, bringing some celery seed for the potato salad.

"I hope you're in the mood to peel some of these suckers," Cynthia said, waving a potato as she swung the door wide, "because—"

"Because what?" Lane smiled and let his eyes roam freely down Cynthia's attire. "You know— you still look great in jeans, Cyn. Turn around."

Cynthia's hand froze on the knob. The hand displaying the potato froze in midair. "What are you doing here?"

Lane frowned. "We agreed. We're going to spend the holiday in Oregon because your family's here. You haven't changed your mind, have you?"

He raised one hand to the doorframe and leaned into her. He was in a relentlessly cheery mood. "You may as well turn around, Cyn. You know you're going to have to walk away from me sometime, and then I'll know what your jeans look like from the back."

Cynthia looked at Lane in amazement. Mr. Smooth was an incarnation she hadn't seen before.

She smiled sweetly. "I walked away ten years ago, and that's when your opinion of my jeans ceased to be an issue." She jerked the door wider, stood to the side and gestured for Lane to walk past her. "Come in."

He grinned and strolled past. The insolent sway

of his hips suggested that he had no doubt that she was watching *his* jeans.

"What's the matter with you today?" she said to his back. "Are you taking testosterone?"

Lane turned around and laughed heartily. "No, I'm just happy." He held out a small jar. "Here. I brought your celery seed."

Cynthia accepted the jar. "You've already been to Mom—to my mother's?"

"Mmm-hmm. I got in early and I didn't see any reason to stay at the motel."

Cynthia didn't say anything. She'd made the motel reservation and had told him of it over the phone when she'd called to firm up his plans. She'd been spending a good deal of time talking herself out of feeling guilty about it ever since. Even now her two empty bedrooms were screaming at her. She focused on reminding herself that he could certainly afford the motel's monthly rate. And he would be able to see Beth whenever he wanted.

Wordlessly, Cynthia turned and walked ahead of Lane into the kitchen, carefully keeping every bit of sway out of her hips.

Lane followed, smiling all the while until he said, "Uh, your mom asked me something I thought I should talk to you about."

Cynthia put the celery seed on the counter and moved to the sink to peel her potato. "Oh?"

"Yeah." Lane picked up a potato. "Here, I'll help. You have another peeler?"

"No." She gripped her peeler more tightly. She did not want to remember Lane's helpfulness. Or the way he'd always kissed her after dinner, grabbed a sponge and pulled her away from the sink, insisting that the person who'd cooked was entitled to rest after dinner. She kept her eyes on the peel that was falling into the sink.

"There really isn't that much to do. What did my mother ask you?"

"Let me do the potatoes, Cyn. I know you must have something else to do."

He pulled the potato and peeler out of her hand. For one moment when his fingers touched hers, Cynthia simply froze. She felt his palm cover the top of her hand. He still had warm palms in winter. Breaking away, she moved quickly to the refrigerator, wishing that she had one of those very, very large kitchens which could accommodate her moving a few yards away from him.

Lane sensed her confusion and liked it. His own reaction was something else again. The tops of her hands felt as soft and delicate as they had ten years ago. They still got cold in the winter, too. Without even thinking, he'd been about to warm her small hands in his. It was a conditioned response to Cynthia's cold hands, but she'd pulled away before he could act. He wondered if there were any divorced people who still felt comfortable warming each other's hands in the winter.

He kept his eyes trained casually on the potato while she worked at the counter behind him.

"It was good to see your mom and stepdad again. Milt hasn't changed much."

"No."

"And Lea looks wonderful. You've got good genes. You'll probably still look great when you're her age."

Cynthia stuck her head in the refrigerator again. Lane heard a muffled "Thanks."

He stopped waffling. Time to get to the point. "Your mother told me that Gwen and Franklin are taking the girls to Portland and Mount Hood for a couple of weeks. She asked me to stay at her place. I said yes."

Lane paused. Cynthia stopped rummaging in the refrigerator. He turned and addressed her back. "I don't want to sit in a motel room by myself when there's family nearby…even ex-family."

Cynthia turned to look at him. She saw no censure—just a steady chocolate-brown gaze which said, *It's Christmas, Cyn.*

For years she'd wondered what holidays were like for him without his family. He had a couple of aunts in Idaho, but he'd rarely spoken about them. He'd never before even suggested that this time of year was difficult for him.

Then again, Cynthia thought as color and heat suffused her face, had she ever asked? He'd always seemed so independent. Her gaze dropped to his knees, and she had a queer, unbidden image of him shopping for jeans alone, the way she shopped for her clothes, always wishing she could turn to someone and say, "What do you think?"

She looked up again. He seemed to be waiting for her okay.

"They're not your ex-family," she said slowly, quietly. "After all, you're still Beth's father."

He smiled and nodded his thanks. He turned back to the sink and started peeling again. "So, tell me. What are we making here?"

Cynthia cringed a little, guiltily. "Potato salad."

"Mmm. I love potato salad." He sounded utterly sincere.

"You hate potato salad!"

He tossed a grin over his shoulder. "You remember. I'm flattered. What else do you remember, Cyn?"

He'd lightened the mood, but he was also baiting her.

"I remember that you're allergic to celery seed. You break out in big ugly hives, if I recall correctly."

Lane looked at the jar on the counter and laughed. "You wouldn't have."

Cynthia shrugged and plopped some mayonnaise into a bowl. "I was considering it."

"You know what I remember?" he asked conversationally. "I remember your face the day we saw the dolphins off Catalina Island. First you had this look of incredible wonder. And then you looked so peaceful. I thought you were so beautiful. You had the same look on your face the day we got married."

His voice had dropped to a quiet tone of reverence. Cynthia didn't move.

He was doing it again, just like he had ten years ago. He was saying all the right things, sucking her into the magic…the realm of possibility.

Damn the men who were magicians.

They were never around when the illusion shattered, and the women were left to pick up the pieces. The women who loved them grew old before their time. They became wary and cautious and cynical when all they wanted to be was young…and naive enough to still believe.

First her father had taught her the lesson, and then Lane had reinforced it.

Henry Gordon James had been a traveling salesman and a magician. Not just the kind of magician who pulled coins out of people's ears, although he did that, too, whenever he could get a gig or an impromptu audience. But Henry Gordon James had been more—he had been one of *life's* magicians, a man who could make the plainest day feel like a trip on the Ferris wheel at the county fair.

Henry had shunned the everyday, never quite getting around to shoveling the snow off the driveway—but he'd made the best snowmen in town. He'd told his two daughters that snowflakes were "the angels sending down Christmas cards," and he'd bought the town's tallest Christmas trees, even though he had owned the shabbiest house on the block.

The girls had worshiped their father, but the magic had worn thin more quickly for Cynthia's mother. By the time Cynthia was seven, the fights had started—long, vitriolic fights that would last far into the night. Then her father would leave, and her mother would do housework with tears in her tired eyes. And Cynthia began to ask questions: "Why are you crying?" "Why does Daddy always go away?" "Why can't he work in the market like Jessica Winkler's dad?"

One night Cynthia had awakened to yet another fight, and this time her mother's voice had risen above the furious, hissing whisper Cynthia had grown used to.

"You could have taken the in-house job at Fortman's. And George Winkler offered you a job at the market. I know because Judy Winkler told me! You want to leave. Admit it! Your family's never been enough for you. For once, admit it!''

Cynthia's father had returned fire in a lower rumble that Cynthia couldn't hear, but he'd left before morning and hadn't returned for several weeks.

The rejection Cynthia felt had been huge, unspeakable. She never told anyone what she'd discovered that night, but she never forgot it, either. Henry Gordon James didn't need his family.

Cynthia's mother had played the hapless victim for the next several years, always waiting for a man who would only hurt her, hurt them all, by not needing them enough. It seemed to Cynthia that the family had lived in limbo during those years, until finally her father had stopped coming back altogether.

Cynthia remembered herself as she'd been before she met Lane—introverted, private, wanting desperately to reach out and ask someone to love her, but fearing in equal proportion that the someone she chose would find it all too easy one day to simply walk away.

And secretly, privately—and hating herself for what she'd perceived to be her weakness—she'd wanted the magic back. Oh, how she'd longed for the magic again! The long, lazy days when her father had brought sunshine to the rainiest afternoon.

Then Lane had come—pulling when she pushed away, making his presence felt and impossible to ignore. He'd brought the magic back. But it hadn't lasted, and the pain of knowing that no matter how much she loved him, no matter how exhilarating and warm and safe every moment in his arms felt, she could not keep his interest. That pain had nearly killed her. No, Cynthia James Lincoln knew, love was never enough.

"Why did you say that, Lane?" Her voice was flat and matter-of-fact. This time she would arm herself to fight the allure by knowing exactly where they both stood.

He faced her. "All I'm saying is that we felt something good for each other then. We should be able to be friendly divorcés now, don't you think? When this month is over, I don't want to go back to the status quo. I think we can do better than that."

The expression in his eyes was frank and questioning. Cynthia wanted to return the favor of his honesty, but more than that she wanted to be honest for her own sake. No more running away from her feelings...or her reasons for wanting to keep her distance.

"I don't think I *want* to do better than the status quo," she said, trying to maintain eye contact when she wanted desperately to focus on a planter or something. "I'm not comfortable with the idea of being part of your life in any concrete way, or of you being part of mine."

Lane put the potato he was still holding onto the counter behind him. He leaned back against the sink, crossed one ankle over the other and his arms across his chest. "Why not?"

"You say you remember a lot of good things. Well, so do I, but I remember the pain, too. I remember how much we hurt each other...how we couldn't help but hurt each other because we wanted different things. What we had—our infatuation— just wasn't enough, and maybe that's not anybody's fault, but I had a lot of expectations about marriage.

The disappointment left too many painful memories.'' She took a slow, shaky breath. ''I don't want to have to relive them every time we talk to each other.''

''Or see each other?''

''If we ever had occasion to see each other, yes.''

Lane nodded. His gaze never left Cynthia's, but his eyes were unreadable. There was a tense moment of silence, during which Cynthia wondered incongruously, ridiculously, if she would still have time to make the potato salad. Lane spoke.

''I asked your stepfather today to forgive me for running out on the job he gave me all those years ago.''

Cynthia looked at him quizzically. ''It never bothered him that much. He forgave you—''

''I know,'' Lane interrupted and, if possible, his brown eyes grew more intense. ''I asked because it needed to be said. Mostly for me, I guess. Now I'm asking you, Cynthia. For whatever we did to each other when we were too young to know better, let's forgive each other and ourselves and be glad that we made a fantastic daughter together. We needed each other for that, at least.''

He uncrossed his legs, uncrossed his arms and pushed away from the sink. His quiet voice enveloped them, making Cynthia's kitchen seem like a more intimate, private room.

''You're the mother of the only child I have,'' he told her, adding silently, *the only child I'm ever likely to have. And I'm the father of your only child, Cyn. We'll always be each other's happiest memories... and our most painful.*

She wasn't ready to hear that, though, so aloud

he said, "I would like to get to know the mother of
the best thing that ever happened to me. I'd like to
know who she is now, and I would like her to know
me, if only so we can finally forgive each other."
He held out his hand. "No strings, Cynthia. Just a
one-month mutual surrender."

Just a mutual surrender. Cynthia heard his words
and took his hand, and she knew already that the
surrender would be hers.

Pulling her hand away from the firm, businesslike
shake, Cynthia turned to the counter. "I'm going to
put these eggs away. I'll make mashed potatoes. As
long as we've declared a truce, it wouldn't be fair
to make you eat potato salad." She laughed a little,
nervously.

Lane took the egg carton from her hands. "On
the contrary, the name of this game is compromise.
I'll eat your potato salad…if you leave out the celery seed."

She nodded. "Deal."

The doorbell rang, and Cynthia glanced at the
clock on her stove. "Oh brother, I'm really running
late. That must be—"

She stopped herself, and Lane looked at her quizzically as he opened a cupboard to find a pot in
which to boil the eggs.

"Who?"

It was Alan, and Cynthia had no reason to feel
guilty, except that she'd invited him to dinner tonight expressly so that she would have a good excuse to keep her distance from Lane.

Lane found a small stainless-steel pot and took it
to the sink to fill it with water. The doorbell rang
again. He raised a questioning brow.

Without saying anything else, she left the kitchen. Alan was waiting beyond her front door with a bouquet of white flowers and a box of pear drops. She hadn't seen him since she'd returned from the book tour.

"Hello, Cynthia." He smiled broadly, and the simple greeting was given more meaning. "I missed you."

Cynthia smiled, exclaimed over the flowers, accepted the candy—which she would shelve with the other boxes he'd given her—and ushered him in.

Alan was wearing trousers and a casual jacket. It occurred to Cynthia that she'd never gone with *him* to pick out clothes, either, or he'd be wearing a different color right now. Navy blue made him appear so sedate.

His kiss was sedate, too, but she knew that his restraint was out of respect for her. Despite Beth's prediction that Alan might be her stepfather by this time next year, Cynthia's relationship with him was as casual as it could be and still be considered dating. Alan let her set the pace.

As he drew away from her, Cynthia gestured to her jeans with the flowers. "I'm sorry I'm not dressed yet. I haven't even finished the potato salad."

"No problem by me. I'm in no hurry. I'll just grab a beer, if that's okay with the lady of the manor." He breezed by her on his way to the kitchen.

"Oh, listen…Alan, uh, I need to tell you…"

Cynthia was still babbling when Alan entered the kitchen and halted so quickly that she nearly tripped on his heels.

"Oh, hi," Alan said slowly, drawing out the words. He pointed a finger at Lane. "You must be..."

"Alan, this is..."

"Cynthia told me you were..."

"Lane got here a little..."

Lane got up from the kitchen table, where he'd made himself right at home with a bottle of the beer Alan wanted. On the table in front of him, there was a small mound of potatoes and a bowl into which he was scraping the peel. He wiped his right hand over his jeans and extended it toward the man who didn't seem to know whether to advance or retreat.

"I'm Lane, the ex. Glad to meet you, Al. Cynthia mentioned you. Did I hear you say you wanted a beer?"

"Uh, yes, I, uh..." Alan pointed to the refrigerator.

"No problem," Lane assured him. "I know where it is."

Reaching into Cynthia's refrigerator, he withdrew a bottle, twisted off the cap and handed it over. "Need a glass, Al?"

Cynthia could see Alan responding like a Pavlovian dog to the unforgivably male baiting. "No, I don't need a glass."

Alan was almost as tall as Lane, and he usually conducted himself with an air of confidence that was admirable. Cynthia felt terrible that she had sprung her ex-husband on him without warning.

"Lane just came over to deliver some celery seed I'm thinking of putting in the potato salad."

Lane shot her a "what'd-I-do?" look. He walked back to his potatoes.

"So, Al, you live in Oregon *and* Washington, hmm? Where do you work?"

Alan cleared his throat and rediscovered his ability to speak in complete sentences. "My business is based here in the Applegate Valley, but we ship throughout the Pacific Northwest."

Lane nodded, then frowned. "And what is it you ship, exactly?"

"Well, we produce and ship many different products, all derived from pears."

"Pears," Lane repeated appreciatively. He had a look of exquisite interest on his face. "Yeah, I remember I ate a lot of pears when I lived in Oregon."

"Yes, Cynthia tells me you live and work in Hollywood now."

Lane chuckled. "Yup. Now I eat a lot of avocados and sprouts."

"Oregon's quite a change from Hollywood. I'm sure you'll miss it."

"Oh, I don't know. It's hard for a place like Hollywood to meet all of an old man's needs."

"Well—" Cynthia stepped in, her voice a little brighter than necessary "—I know that I need to get ready, and, Lane, I'm sure you want to get back to Beth."

"Actually, she's playing with her cousins." He caught the exasperated look Cynthia shot him. "But I do need to get back." He started to leave, then paused again. "Oh, speaking of needs, you wouldn't happen to have any chocolate in the house, Cyn?"

"Chocolate? No."

"I didn't think so. You never did crave it."

Cynthia laughed. "Actually, it's funny you should say that. I've been buying chocolate like crazy lately. I bought a pound last week. I'm ashamed to say I ate it all.''

Lane smiled benevolently. ''Nothing to be ashamed of.'' He addressed Cynthia's friend. ''You eat a lot of chocolate, Al?''

Alan considered the question. ''A fair amount of it, yes. We have some chocolate made with pears that I do indulge in.''

Lane clapped Alan heartily on the shoulder. ''Well, good, good. You keep it up.''

Ignoring their puzzlement, Lane said goodbye and left Cynthia's house feeling better about his future than he had in a long, long time.

Chapter Six

Dinner was less than a triumph.

The potato salad had been scrapped, so Cynthia made cottage fries when she got to her mother's. Lane was visibly pleased by the change in menu, but the time Cynthia spent frying potatoes in her mother's kitchen left Alan stuck in the living room with Lane.

Fortunately there were enough other relatives to keep the conversation moving—and to keep it safely banal.

Gwen—six and a half months pregnant—was there with Franklin and their daughters. Cynthia's stepfather, Milton, was present and never at a loss for words, even if his conversation revolved mostly around electrical appliances. Lea bustled around, making sure everyone had enough to eat and drink, and Cynthia's aunt Fanny was there to make sure that the evening wasn't *too* tame.

Aunt Fanny was Lea's sister, but she was as dif-

ferent from Lea—and Cynthia—as light is from
dark. At fifty-six years of age, Fanny dressed like a
twenty-year-old at the Hard Rock Café—and looked
good. She favored spandex leggings, multicolored
gauzy blouses and jewelry that somehow managed
to tinkle even when she was sitting still. Her hair
was short, curly and strawberry blond.

Fanny was between her fourth and fifth husbands
at present and had just returned from a two-week
stay in Cancún.

Cynthia had not known her grandparents, and she
never ceased to wonder how one set of parents could
produce such vastly different siblings. Lea was as
grounded as Fanny was flighty.

The one thing each relative had in common was
a sincere delight that Lane was visiting. They grilled
him endlessly about Hollywood and moviemaking
and movie stars, most of whom Lane said he'd seen
but hadn't really met. He didn't go to many parties,
he said. He just wrote scripts.

Alan glowered and said a few words about pears.

Cynthia was glad when the evening ended.

Lane went back to his motel. He would move into
Lea's in two days, when Gwen and her family left
for Portland.

Alan took Cynthia and Beth home.

Beth ran upstairs to her room almost immediately.
Cynthia offered to make coffee, and even though
they'd both had their fill of it at her mother's, Alan
accepted.

They sat on Cynthia's old plaid couch in the living room. It was time to talk, but Cynthia didn't
know how to get started. She did know that Alan

deserved some reassurance, some signal that Lane's visit here was for Beth's sake only.

Alan graciously solved the problem of where to begin.

"Well, your ex-husband's quite a guy."

Cynthia smiled apologetically. "I know it was a little overwhelming with everybody fawning over him like that. The last time they saw him, he was working as a clerk in a record store. You need to understand—"

"I do understand." Alan ran a hand through his sandy hair, then leaned his elbows on his knees. "Hell, I was tempted to ask him questions myself. I know it's exciting for them to have a minor celebrity in the family."

Cynthia frowned slightly. She'd been about to thank him for his patience and understanding, but she didn't like the way he'd said "minor."

"I don't know if I'd call Lane a *minor* celebrity, exactly. I mean, he has written some very successful movies."

"I know." Alan's laugh was completely good-natured. She really couldn't find fault with it. "But so has Sylvester Stallone. That doesn't make him Shakespeare."

He leaned back and put his arm around Cynthia's shoulders. "You said yourself that his screenplays aren't grounded in reality."

"I've really only seen one of them." Cynthia pushed a stray blond hair behind her ear. She was lying—she'd seen them all, actually; one about young lovers on a cross-country trip she'd seen twice.

Alan sighed. "Okay, I didn't mean to make you feel like you had to defend him."

He shifted on the couch, turning his body toward Cynthia and keeping his arm behind her, just brushing her hair and neck.

Cynthia always enjoyed her evenings with Alan because they invariably ended on a quiet, relaxing note. She sat on the couch now, her hands folded primly in her lap, and wondered if that feeling was about to come to an end.

"You've always been honest about not wanting a more...full relationship." His fingers toyed with a strand of her hair. "And I've respected that. But now I need to know how you feel about me—how you feel about our relationship."

It was a fair question. More than fair. She had known Alan for three years. She'd been dating him—casually, she kept reminding herself—for over one year. It was so very reasonable of him to want to know where they were going.

Alan spoke again before she could answer. "I know you have strong opinions about the type of relationship that works in the long run." His free hand closed over the hands that were clasped in her lap. "I have opinions, too. And I think we have what it takes. We're both responsible and grounded. We're in sync." He smiled, and the pressure on her hands increased. "What I need to know is...is your ex-husband in our way?"

Cynthia's gaze, which had been meandering safely around the room, now flew to his face. "No...of course not."

Alan smiled. "I'm relieved. He may have been

caviar, Cynthia, but I'm meat and potatoes. I have the substance it takes to make it work.''

It was what Cynthia had been telling herself for a long time, but, somehow, hearing Alan say it made her feel resentful. She tried to shake the feeling off. She didn't want to be alone forever, she knew that much. And Alan was the type of man she could trust to be steadfast, stable. Her smile wobbled only a bit as she said, ''Maybe we could see each other more often, Alan. After Christmas we could—''

''*Before* Christmas, Cynthia. Tomorrow night is the tour of homes. I'd like to take you and Beth. It'll be a quiet evening, but at least we'll get some time together.'' He smiled convincingly. ''I haven't seen you much for the past month.''

Cynthia wondered if she should make plans for Beth when Lane was in town. She wondered if she should make plans for herself when she'd promised Beth a month of family activities. Then she dismissed the worry as unreasonable. There would be nights apart, that was only realistic. And she had a life to consider after this month was over.

''We'd love to go with you.''

Upstairs, sitting on the carpeted landing, Beth gently and meditatively tapped her feet. She got up after a moment and returned to her room, pondering deeply. She didn't even feel guilty about eavesdropping. She'd heard the old expression, ''All's fair...''

''Pregnant women get all the breaks,'' Cynthia grumbled good-naturedly as she dropped into a lawn chair next to her sister.

Gwen grinned around a mouthful of root-beer-flavored popcorn and rubbed her big tummy. "Ain't it the truth?"

She'd been sitting on her chair on their mother's redwood deck for the past hour, watching the girls play touch football with Franklin and Lane, while Cynthia helped their mother shred cabbage for red cabbage slaw. She held the popcorn out to her sister.

"Want some?"

Cynthia grimaced at the sickly sweet popcorn. "Ugh!" She shuddered. "How can you eat that all day long?"

"Same way I eat everything all day long. It's one of the perks of pregnancy. Besides, I vary it. This morning I had garlic popcorn."

"Oh, please!" Cynthia begged for mercy. "That poor child is going to have indigestion till she's twelve."

"*He*," Gwen corrected, wincing as her two daughters went for a full tackle on one play. "I haven't told Franklin yet, but we're having a boy, thank God. If I had to watch him teach another one of my darling daughters how to play football and hook worms, I think I'd go crazy."

Cynthia grinned. Gwen's daughters, Allison and Nikki, were adorable bundles of energy who adored their daddy. They were eight and six, respectively, and badly wanted a baby brother to fawn over.

"When are you going to tell Franklin you're having a boy?"

"Right after they cut the umbilical cord," Gwen said dryly. "I still have three months to go. I don't want him preening all through the holidays. But I might tell him in Portland if he plays his cards right and takes me to a lovely little French restaurant I've heard about. All those rich sauces…mmm!''

Cynthia laughed. "I still can't believe you're traveling right now. Isn't it uncomfortable?''

"It'll be more uncomfortable after the baby. I probably won't get to leave the house again until I'm sixty. I want to take advantage of having only two children to cart around. Besides, Franklin really is wonderful to me. He keeps me relaxed…and he keeps one suitcase fully stocked with popcorn.'' Gwen wiggled her brows like she'd just divulged racy information about their sex life.

Cynthia shook her head. She enjoyed watching Franklin—and Lane—with the girls.

"Franklin is a good father,'' she said.

"So's Lane.'' Gwen sensed the direction of her sister's thoughts. "We're both lucky in that respect.''

Cynthia nodded, watching Lane huddle with Beth as they plotted their strategy against Franklin and his daughters. As they broke the huddle and Beth trotted off to her position, Lane glanced up. His eyes met Cynthia's, and for a moment his gaze did not waver. She was about to look away, when he raised a hand and smiled in greeting.

How strange and how new this all was, Cynthia thought as she watched Lane move to his position and signal to Beth. As a single mother, she hadn't been able to watch the playtimes between her child and the child's father. She'd missed all the big changes—and the subtle ones—in their relationship. Before today she'd had no idea they felt so comfortable together, or that they laughed so easily at each other's jokes. Or that they each brushed hair out of their eyes with the same hand in exactly the same way, always pushing from right to left.

Gwen's voice seemed to come from far away. "What are you doing for Beth's birthday?"

Cynthia looked at her sister and shrugged. "You'll be back by then, so I'd like to have a party, but...I thought I'd better talk over my plans with Lane. I mean, since he's here...he may have some ideas for something special."

"Hmm." Gwen nodded. "You think you and Lane will stay in contact now once the holidays are over?"

It was clear from the rest of the family's attitude that they already assumed she would stay in touch with her ex-husband.

"I don't know," Cynthia told Gwen honestly. "He wants to."

"I knew he would." Gwen put her popcorn on the little table by the side of her chair. Out of the blue, she asked, "Do you ever wonder where Dad is?"

Cynthia looked as startled as she felt. "*Our* dad?"

"Yes."

Their absent father was the one thing the sisters never discussed. Whether to spare their mother's feelings or each other's or their own, they had for years avoided even the mention of his name. He'd left for good when Cynthia was sixteen and Gwen was twelve. And that had been the end of him, as far as Cynthia was concerned.

"No," she answered her sister. "I don't think about him."

"Oh, bull," Gwen challenged bluntly. "You

never think about him? You never wonder if he's well...or even still alive?''

"I wasn't the one who left without leaving a forwarding address.''

''The phone rang here the other day,'' Gwen said quietly, reflectively. ''I picked it up and there was silence. I must have said hello five times. For a minute I wondered if maybe...''

She let the thought trail off. She didn't have to finish it. For years, Cynthia had wondered the same thing every time the phone rang: *Maybe it's him. He's checking to see how we are. He wants to hear my voice again. He's being held hostage in another state, but he got to a phone and was able to make the call right before they found him and disconnected the line.*

She said nothing as Gwen continued. ''I especially think about him around Christmas. Remember Elsbeth the Christmas tree? Dad let us feed her marshmallows because we thought she looked hungry.'' Gwen laughed. ''Big, white, fat marshmallows stuck on to the tree between the tinsel. And the hand tricks he could do! Remember how he could make his fingers look like they were growing?''

Yes, Gwen, I remember, Cynthia thought but would not say aloud. I remember Elsbeth, and the marshmallows and the magic tricks. I remember his smile, and I remember what he told me when I asked him where snow came from.

It's the angels sending down Christmas cards, Cinnamon Girl. It's the angels sending us Christmas cards.

No, she could not forget a life that had seemed magical, no matter how much she wanted to.

Neither woman spoke for a moment, one content to sit with her thoughts, the other acutely discontent, but unable to do anything about it. They were both relieved when Fanny came swooping out of the house.

"Good Lord, Guinevere, are you still eating those horse droppings? I've never tasted anything so cloying." Fanny grabbed the bag off the table and rolled the cellophane tightly. She looked out into the yard. "Nice buns, those men of yours have. Very nice. Rocco, who may be your new uncle, has lovely buns, too. Too bad he couldn't be here, but he has a good business in Cancún, selling trinkets and T-shirts. He does a fine Christmas trade."

The sisters looked at each other and shared a smile. Now they knew what Fanny was giving them for Christmas. Five years ago when she'd married the ski instructor, they'd all gotten free skiing lessons.

The football game ended, and three shouting, whooping children clambered onto the deck. Two tired, sweaty men dragged up after them.

"Well, I think we showed 'em what's what," Lane panted as Franklin tiredly bent to kiss his wife's head.

"Uh-uh, didn't show us anything!" Nikki crowed.

"Daddy says we beat the pants off of 'em," Allison told her mother proudly.

Gwen smiled beatifically at her husband. "Nice move, Daddy. Instill in them that competitive spirit." She gave clean up orders to her children.

"You two go inside and try to blast some of that mud off before lunch."

At the mention of lunch, the two girls ran into the house, shouting for their cousin to come with them. "C'mon, Beth!"

"I'll be there in a minute." Beth turned to her mother. "Hey, Mom…" She leaned into the chair Cynthia was sitting on.

"Yes, sweetpea?"

Beth smiled at the endearment she loved best. She bent forward to touch her mother's nose with her own. "How about if you and Dad and I go to a movie, sweetpea?" She returned the endearment as she always did.

Cynthia tried to keep her features calm and agreeable. The family holiday was beginning. "Sure. When?"

"Tonight. There are double features in—"

"We can't tonight, Beth."

Cynthia braved a refusal in front of Lane and the three family members who were standing by. Only Lane had the grace to appear utterly casual as he rolled the football between his hands. The others were listening to her answer with an interest they didn't bother to mask.

"We're going on the tour of homes with Alan. He was nice enough to invite us, and since we caused him to alter his plans this holiday, I thought it would be nice if we spent tonight with him."

Not at all certain what to expect from her daughter where this family holiday was concerned, Cynthia prepared for anything, including a tantrum. She did not expect to see Beth's face wreathed in a bright, excited smile.

"That's great!" Beth enthused guilelessly. "Dad's never been on a home tour, I bet." She turned to her father. "You'll love it, Dad. We walk through the homes after dark, and they're all decorated for the holidays. And a few of the houses are really, really old. It's spooky. You could write a movie about it."

Cynthia opened her mouth, but knew nothing would come out. Lane smiled, perfectly happy with the change in plans.

"Great. So, these are actually private homes?"

"Uh-huh. It costs ten bucks. Two bucks a house." Beth nodded, delighted.

"Well, Cyn, that's awfully nice of Alan." Lane tossed the football lightly into the air, catching it in one hand. "Remind me to thank him."

"You're welcome."

Alan stared over Lane's shoulder, sullenly accepting his thanks, but refusing to make eye contact with him or, at the moment, with anyone else.

Cynthia felt unutterably guilty, but knew that she would have felt even worse had Lane been left at home. She looked at him now and thought he looked rather cheerful. And—she had to admit—rather handsome. He was wearing a down vest and a handsome sweater of forest green with a wide blue stripe and white snowflakes that emphasized his broad shoulders and muscular chest. And he was, clearly, ready to have a good time.

They were standing outside Cynthia's house and were deciding now whose car to take. Lane had rented a compact, much more sedate than his cherry-red Saab. Alan had a dark blue luxury sedan and insisted on driving. Cynthia sat in the front with him and read the tour map.

As they moved through the first four houses, Alan's mood lightened. Lane had so far left them alone. In each house, he took Beth's hand and told Cynthia they'd meet back in the home's entry at a designated time. Then he led Beth off to explore and left Cynthia with Alan. If their paths crossed as they went through the homes, Lane would offer some little pleasantry about an attractive bathroom or the "great Berber carpeting in the master bedroom," and then move on.

Cynthia was going nuts. She'd wanted him to keep his distance. But now, every time she went into a room Lane had already explored, his presence assailed her. She smelled the woodsy aftershave he used. She wondered if he liked beveled mirrors and whether he preferred walnut to English pine. In each room, she cursed herself for her wayward thoughts and then—in that ironic way of women who were being ignored by men—went right on thinking them.

The last house on the tour was a three-story, queenly old Victorian built in 1888. There were wonderful surprises in every room. Incredible woodwork, odd little nooks and crannies, and beautiful furniture, much of which had been in the house for almost a century.

Harold and Trixie Baker were the proud owners. They were both in their mid-eighties, and the house had been in Trixie's family since her grandfather had won it in a horseshoe game in 1894. Harold and Trixie loved to open their home and were always present during the tour hours. Tonight Harold was wearing an electric-blue sweatshirt that boasted

"Octogenarians do it slowly—they have to." Trixie kept looking at the shirt and giggling, "Oh, Harold!"

Cynthia and Alan were exploring the kitchen when Beth came running up.

"You've gotta come see the basement," she enthused. "It's huge! There's a wine cellar, and everything looks real old and spooky."

Cynthia shuddered. Where there were basements, there were spiders.

Beth was already pulling Alan by the hand, and Cynthia was glad to see it. Beth had been ignoring them as effectively as Lane had all evening.

"You two go ahead," Cynthia urged. "I'll keep looking around up here."

"Okay," Beth agreed readily. "Come on, Alan. Wait till you see it. The wine bottles are really dusty, and there are cobwebs...."

Cynthia cringed and stepped into the hall. The room next to the kitchen came as a complete and wonderful surprise. It was a minilibrary, filled from floor to ceiling with books, almost all of them older than Cynthia. All the wood moldings in the small room were exquisitely carved, and there was a wide, welcoming chair near a window which overlooked a lighted mossy brick patio.

Cynthia crossed the threshold and knew instantly that of all the rooms in all the houses, this was the one she liked best. The chair was so old that there was a deep, permanent indentation in the seat cushion which told of all the people who had spent hours reading books here and adding to the collection. This room was history, family, permanence—all the things Cynthia loved best and wanted most.

She was lost in the perusal of a section of the library that was devoted to Mark Twain, when a voice spoke softly behind her.

"Some of those are first editions."

Cynthia felt warmth tingling along her neck. It crept up the back of her head and down her right shoulder. *Lane.* He was standing a couple of feet behind her. It always felt like this. She could feel him touching her even when his hands hadn't left his sides.

She turned around, stuffing her hands in her pockets so she wouldn't be able to fidget. The wall lamp above the chair cast a warm, honey-colored glow behind Lane. He stood with his hands in his vest pockets. His thick hair was mussed slightly from the chill and the breeze outside, but the threads of gold were visible in the light. He was looking at her, not at the books, and his gaze was, as usual, unwavering. There was so much strength in his face. Suddenly she remembered with absolute clarity what his tanned cheek felt like after a shave—smooth and warm with a texture and scent that was all male.

She wanted to stop remembering. She *had* to stop remembering. She wanted permanence. She wanted forever. She wanted a library filled with books the whole family had read and would pass on through generations; she wanted cribs with hand-me-down quilts; and she wanted to come through the door of a library like this and know he'd be sitting in the chair. She wanted someone to need her as much as she needed him.

That man wasn't Lane. Lane had left once. And what had hurt more than anything, more than his leaving, was how easy the decision to leave had been.

Cynthia pressed her fists down into her pockets and stood straighter. "Where's Beth?"

His voice was still quiet.

"I don't know. Roaming around somewhere, I imagine."

"She must be in the basement still."

Lane nodded. "She got a kick out of all the dusty bottles." He took a single step toward her. "Thank you for letting me come along tonight. I don't do much of this in L.A."

"What *do* you do in L.A.?" The words were out before she knew it. Someday she would have to teach her tongue how to behave.

Lane took another step toward her. His brown eyes were quizzical. "What do you think I do?"

Cynthia shrugged inside the collar of her coat. *Play tennis. Date young actresses like that redhead you were photographed with before our divorce was even final.*

Lane had sold his first script shortly after Cynthia had served him with the divorce papers. He'd been a hot property after that—fashionably young, handsome, talented. He'd received more publicity than his movie had.

When Cynthia failed to answer Lane out loud, he took one last step, which brought him a whisper away. "I work, Cynthia. I write and sometimes I jog, and I go to boring parties when my agent tells me I have to make contacts I'll probably never use. I spend a lot of time at my house, and I go for long drives along the coast or in the canyon when I'm lonely. There's something about a canyon that makes loneliness feel right.''

Lonely. Cynthia heard the word, but didn't quite believe it. *You've never before told me that you get lonely. Not once.*

Cynthia wanted to ask him when he got lonely, for how long...and why. She wanted to run from the room before she could utter another word and before he could tell her anything else.

Lane held Cynthia's gaze with his own. Her eyes were still as green. And she still reminded him of an emerald-eyed doe, wary and vulnerable in the same glance. Looking somehow like she needed him—and looking very much like she wished she didn't.

Ask me, Cynthia. Ask me why I'm lonely. God, just trust me one more time. This time, I won't abuse it.

Lane started to lean toward her, and that's when she moved. She walked rapidly to the door, fighting the need to take off her wool coat before she suffocated from the heat that was wholly internal.

''Cyn.'' Lane's voice stopped her when she was just inside the doorway.

She was standing on the left side of the threshold; he came to stand on the right.

''I wasn't honest with you about something when we were in L.A.,'' he said. ''I'd like to tell you the truth now.''

Cynthia frowned. ''What is it?''

''I lied about Vicki. She's not my lover. We've never even dated. You mentioned Alan and the San Juan Islands, and I got jealous and came up with someone of my own. I haven't dated anyone in a long, long time.''

Cynthia's heart began to thump rhythmically and quickly, at a pace she could feel. He shouldn't have found it necessary to tell her. She shouldn't care.

He leaned toward her again, but this time she couldn't have moved if he'd yelled fire.

''There's something else I should tell you,'' he said, pointing up to the top of the doorframe.

Cynthia lifted her eyes. There was a green sprig taped to the wood.

''It's mistletoe,'' Lane told her, breathing the words close to her face.

Cynthia's face was still upturned, her eyes still glued to the mistletoe when Lane's lips met hers. Her eyes closed without any instruction from her mind, and when the pressure of his kiss nudged her head back, she lifted it forward, pressing her lips more firmly to his. She felt his chin graze hers. Their noses touched.

The sensitivity of their lips was amazing…and excruciating. She'd almost forgotten that a kiss—just a kiss—could feel so good.

And it could make you want so much more.

Lane pulled away gently, and Cynthia became aware of voices heading their way. She also became aware that Lane was holding the long wool scarf she'd thrown around the collar of her coat. He hadn't touched her, really, during the kiss; he'd buried his hands in the folds of her scarf.

''I knew you'd love this room, Cyn. You do, don't you?''

Before she could answer the question he'd murmured, two elderly people came around the corner, stopping when they saw Cynthia and Lane standing in the doorway.

"Oh, excuse us," Harold Baker said in his reedy voice. "Didn't mean to disturb you. The wife and I just thought we'd try out the mistletoe."

Trixie Baker giggled from beneath the skinny arm Harold laid across her shoulder.

Cynthia couldn't summon a single word.

Slowly, Lane let go of her scarf and drew away. The deep breath he took before addressing the Bakers was the one indication that he was as affected by the kiss as she was.

"Time for us to get going, anyway," Lane said, relinquishing his spot under the mistletoe as Cynthia scooted past the Bakers with a garbled "Excuse me" and headed down the hall.

Lane nodded at the elderly couple, winked at Mr. Baker, and headed after Cynthia.

Harold Baker pulled his wife of sixty-five years into his arms. "Ready to neck, Mrs. Baker?"

"Yes, I am, Mr. Baker."

"Whatever made you think of mistletoe, Trix?" Harold asked as he lowered his head to hers.

"I didn't," she admitted, gazing into the face she knew so well. She could trace every line with her eyes closed. "That young man pulled it out of his pocket and asked me if he could hang it up. I said sure, as long as he left it for us when he was through."

"You're a smart woman, Trixie. And that's a very sexy idea."

"Oh, Harold…" Trixie giggled.

Lane found Cynthia again in the foyer. Alan and

Beth were already there. Lane held out his hand to the other man.

"Alan, thank you. This was the best evening I've had in years."

Alan looked at him dubiously. "You've got to be kidding. With the parties you must go to?"

Lane made brief eye contact with Cynthia. "Believe me," he said simply, "this was the best."

He felt only vaguely guilty for taking advantage of the evening the other man had planned...and for stepping in, as it were, on what was supposed to have been the other man's date. It was true that he had lost Cynthia fair and square. It was just as true that he was going to get her back...fair or not. It would mean the end of Alan's relationship with Cynthia. But Cynthia had been his wife before she became Alan's date. She would be his wife again. It was written...in their lips, in their eyes, in the stars. She had always been his. He knew it now, at last.

"Listen," Lane said, "I saw a little bakery in town. Let me take you all out for dessert."

"Oh, boy, great! I want an apple fritter."

Lane smiled at his daughter. Subterfuge was coming all too easily to her.

Alan offered no protest, and Cynthia wasn't speaking at all, so they piled into Alan's car one more time and drove down to Main Street.

Main Street in Jacksonville—only a few blocks long, but rich in history and atmosphere—was all dressed up for Christmas. Big red bows, fat green boughs and sparkling lights decorated each shop in the small Victorian town.

There was a horse and carriage ready to ferry people through the streets, a stand advertising hot apple cider and hot cocoa for a dollar, and another stand where warm chestnuts could be purchased for the walk around town. Jacksonville's motto was "Our present to you is our past."

The bakery was warm and cozy, with a tempting selection of desserts.

The three adults drank coffee and Beth chose hot chocolate. They took their drinks to a table, then ordered a fruit tart for Alan and sticky apple fritters for Lane and Beth. Cynthia didn't want dessert, and she refused the bite of apple fritter Lane offered her as though she suspected it was poisoned. The thought of eating something his tanned fingers had touched or his teeth had bitten into seemed unbearably intimate. She sat uncomfortably until the desserts and coffee were finished.

Lane and Beth were the first two to the door. As Beth pushed the door open, she glanced up, then pointed and exclaimed happily, "Look, Dad, mistletoe!"

Lane looked up. "Why so it is, Bethie. Bad luck to ignore it. Give your old man a kiss."

He leaned down and Beth kissed him loudly on the cheek. He returned the favor, then rose and held the door while she skipped through it. Cynthia was standing right behind them.

"After you," Lane said, and after a slight hesitation Cynthia attempted to dart past.

"Oops!" He held her arm with his left hand. "Almost forgot." He bent forward and gave her a quick, soft kiss that left Beth glowing, Cynthia more dazed than before, and Alan furious. Lane smiled into Cynthia's face. "I don't need any bad luck," he said by way of explanation.

Cynthia scuttled out the door. Both Alan and Lane attempted to follow her and wound up crowding the doorway at the same time. They glared at each other in a standoff. Lane glanced up at the mistletoe, glanced back at Alan and raised an eyebrow in question.

More furious than before, Alan growled, "No thanks," and stormed out the door.

Lane shrugged, turned to the two women who were watching from behind the counter and waved.

As they watched him leave, the bespectacled older woman turned to her friend. "What made you get mistletoe this year?"

The other gray-haired lady shook her head. "I didn't. The man doin' all the kissin' come in this afternoon and asked if he could put it up."

A half hour later, Lane was on his way to the motel, Beth was taking a bath, and Cynthia was standing at her front door with Alan. There was no mistletoe.

"Well," Alan said, looking at the blond woman before him with a mixture of irritation and regret, "I guess this is the part where I say, 'Gee, it's been fun, but it's not me you really want....'" His short laugh held no humor.

"Alan—"

"Please—" he held up his hand "—let me finish. I love a good cliché." In the time that he'd known Cynthia, he'd never seen her look so confused, and it softened his anger somewhat.

"If it were just your ex-husband's feelings I had

to contend with, I…well, I wouldn't contend with them. I'd ignore them. But there's a reason you've been holding me off for so long. His name is Lane. I'm going to spend Christmas in Washington, after all," he told her, noting her look of dismay, but not considering it in his decision. "Whatever it takes to get him out of your system…I hope you do it."

Cynthia watched Alan's face, seeing the regret and the resignation. She felt, she thought, the same emotions—and resignation was the stronger of the two. She also felt frightened.

She couldn't remember a time when she'd kissed him and felt passion, or even desire. She had no memory of kissing *anyone* and wanting it to go on forever—anyone except Lane.

The entire premise of her book, the philosophy of the group she had founded, was based on the belief that passion was not the glue which held relationships together. And that addiction to passion often kept people stuck in unhealthy relationships.

With Alan she had the chance to have the stable, secure comradeship she craved. Being independent and choosing to be alone for the next thirty or forty years were two totally different things.

Desire can be cultivated.

Wasn't that also part of her philosophy?

Alan opened the front door and stepped outside. "Goodbye, Cynthia."

He was starting down her walkway when she called to him. Without taking a moment to think about what she was doing, Cynthia threw her arms around Alan's neck, pressed herself into his coat and found his mouth with hers.

Startled, Alan stood still for a moment, then put

his gloved hands on her shoulders and kissed her back. Their chins touched. Their noses touched.

Nothing happened.

Cynthia knew it, and Alan knew it.

Maybe it's our coats, Cynthia thought briefly, desperately. *We can't feel each other....*

But she and Lane had had their coats on, too. The hope that she could create a spark of desire with Alan fluttered and died, and they pulled apart, more resigned than before.

Cynthia felt that she should apologize, but Alan saved her that embarrassment.

"Goodbye, Cynthia," he said again with the ghost of a smile.

He walked to his car, and Cynthia returned to the house. She shut the door and listened for Beth. Music was still playing from the cassette player Beth had taken into the bathroom, and Cynthia was relieved that Beth hadn't come downstairs to witness the awkwardness between herself and Alan.

The handling of dates in front of her daughter had never been a problem for Cynthia. She'd been on so few.

Still wearing her coat, Cynthia collapsed onto the couch. She toyed with the scarf around her neck, absently at first, but soon the memory of Lane's hands, Lane's mouth, Lane's scent assailed her.

She was hopeless. She was more physically aroused just thinking about him than she had been with anybody else in the last ten years. She needed her support group. She needed their strength and their reassurance. She would go to a meeting tomorrow night. Because right now all she wanted was to go to Lane's motel and find the magic again in

his arms—the future, the past and the inevitable pain
be damned.

If she'd gone to his motel, he wouldn't have been
there. If, on the other hand, she'd stepped farther
outside, she might have noticed the blue rental car
parked across the street. And the man sitting in the
driver's seat, rubbing his head.

Lane was angry. Hitting his head on the steering
column had upset him, but not as much as the sight
of Cynthia flinging herself around Alan's neck.

He stared out the windshield into the black night.
Tree branches, silhouetted by the moon and the dark
sky, hung over the street.

As dark as it was, he'd still thought it best to duck
when Alan had walked toward his car. He'd hit his
head on the way back up.

How foolish, how egotistical of him to drive back
here, assuming that Cynthia would have dispatched
Alan immediately. He'd intended to ring her doorbell with the excuse that they really needed to discuss Beth's birthday.

The truth was that he simply needed to be near
Cynthia for a few more moments. He needed the
reassurance that the closeness of her body and the
sound of her voice could give him.

Because he was going to change his life for her.

To live as Cynthia's husband, he had to work on
their relationship...as he hadn't had the guts to work
on it before.

There was much he would have to tell Cynthia,
much he would have to explain, and it wasn't going

to be easy. He had no practice in being honest about being afraid.

Admitting that tonight was best left as it was, Lane turned the key in the ignition and drove back to his motel.

Chapter Seven

"Hi. I'm Suzanne G., compulsive romantic."

The young woman raised her hand and waved hello.

People around the room nodded and smiled. Together they chorused back, "Hi, Suzanne."

They were seated in a circle, on folding chairs. The walls of the room were peach, the carpeting a deeper russet, and there was a large green chalkboard on which someone had written, "Romantics Anonymous meeting here, 7:30 p.m." A handwritten sign on the door said the same thing and added the welcome, "Come on in."

This was the least formal of the R.A. chapters in the area. There were only thirteen members, and only seven to eight usually showed up on any given night. There was time, therefore, for several people to speak during each session and time to open the floor for discussion, if desired, so that each person could get the other members' feedback.

Cynthia looked around the room with fondness and a sense of gratitude. A few of these people were the "originals," the first to respond to her notice of a support group forming for people who needed help letting go of unhealthy relationships. That first group had met for the first time almost seven years ago. They had helped Cynthia get on with her life, and she liked to think she'd helped them, as well.

Suzanne Gentry was one of the newer members. She was preparing to speak during the "open pitch" portion of the meeting.

Suzanne was pretty and sweet and rarely without a smile—even when she was crying. And she'd had a lot to cry about lately, Cynthia reflected, watching her push at the bangs of her Princess Di haircut, her trademark gesture before she started to speak.

"First I just want to say I'm really happy that Cynthia is back from her book tour." There was a rowdy round of applause. Suzanne smiled at Cynthia. "We missed you."

Suzanne took a cleansing breath, the way one of their guest therapists had shown them, and straightened the pink waist-length cardigan she wore over her jeans.

"Well, it's been a really full week for me. Ten people were laid off where I work, and I was one of them." Murmurs of condolence went up around the circle. "But they're keeping us through January 31, so at least it won't completely mess up Christmas."

Suzanne's ever-present smile was at the ready. "The baby's teething, so he's been crying a lot, and I haven't gotten much sleep, and my best friend just told me that she's moving to Wisconsin." Here the tears started to gather in Suzanne's trusting blue eyes. "I think this has all made me feel really vulnerable...and really alone...because I've been thinking a lot about Chad."

Cynthia listened with a heart full of empathy and a growing sense of pride as the young woman spoke so openly about her continuing love for the man who had repeatedly betrayed her trust.

In Suzanne's own words, Chad was "a stud." He was handsome and romantic and told Suzanne how much he loved her. He had also cheated on her a month or so before their wedding. Suzanne had forgiven him—only to find him in bed with a bridesmaid a few hours before the rehearsal dinner. She'd canceled the wedding, returned all the presents and then had forgiven him again long enough to become pregnant. This time he'd waited until right *after* the wedding to sleep with her cousin. Suzanne had divorced him over a year ago, but the feelings hadn't ended. And, as always when you believed you were truly in love, the feelings weren't all bad. They were, however, bad for her, so Suzanne came to Romantics Anonymous to learn which feelings to act on and which to work through.

When she was through speaking, Suzanne asked for comments and received an earful of them. Everyone had an opinion, and the comments ranged from lovingly supportive to the suggestion that she draw a picture of Chad nude and throw darts at it.

That little gem came from Millie, a fifty-year-old divorcée who had been the first to respond to Cynthia's notice seven years ago.

Snapping the cinnamon gum she was never without, Millie said, "It's harder when you've got a kid...you know, something that actually looks like him.'' She shook her head and turned to Cynthia. ''You tell her, honey. You had a kid when Prince Charming took the family jewels to California.''

Nothing Millie said ever offended Cynthia. She had been there when Millie had cried every night for months because her alcoholic then-husband had told her he didn't love her anymore.

Smiling at Suzanne, who was still wiping tears from her eyes, Cynthia nodded. ''I did have a child when Lane and I divorced. It does get easier, Suzanne, you just...''

Cynthia trailed off before she could utter the platitude about taking one day at a time. It was good advice, but who was she to give advice right now? She was still in love with the man she had divorced ten years ago so she could get on with her life. How far, then, had she gotten?

The others were looking at her expectantly, wondering why she paused.

She lowered her gaze a moment and shook her head. Her hair was in a loose braid tonight, and she was wearing a cranberry-colored sweater with tiny embroidered roses. She had dark blue jeans on, and to Millie she didn't look much older than she had that first night, when they had all sat around wondering how—or *if*—they should begin.

''Go ahead, honey,'' Millie urged softly, realizing it was time for Cynthia to be supported.

Cynthia glanced gratefully at Millie, then raised her eyes to the rest of the group. She took a deep breath.

''I'm in contact with my ex-husband again. In fact, he's here in Oregon,'' she said, noting the surprise on one or two faces. "I hadn't seen him in ten years," she added for the benefit of those who were newer to the group, "and I think I'm still attracted to him—I *know* I'm still attracted to him." She shook her head in wonder at the irony. "I really believed I'd moved on a long time ago. But now that he's here...I know I've never felt very much for other men. And I keep saying that we can create sexual feelings when the rest of a relationship is strong...but I don't seem to have those feelings for anybody but Lane. Now, when I'm with him, I feel more...alive...than I have in a long time."

Her gaze settled on her own knees. She spoke softly and as honestly as she could. "I don't want us to hurt each other again, like we did last time. We just couldn't give each other what we needed.

"I think," Cynthia said, her brows coming together and her lips compressing as she tried not to cry, but failed, "I think that what bothers me the most...still...is that he let me divorce him...when I loved him so much."

The people around the circle were silent and still. She had voiced the one thing they feared most. If even the younger and stronger among them could go on loving one person above all, then when would the pain ever end? The answer, of course, was what most of them had already discovered: the pain didn't end—it simply changed and it softened, and you worked your way through it. Watching Cynthia reminded them of how human they all were. Sometimes you were stuck with your feelings whether you liked them or not.

"Maybe you need a little safe sex, honey," Millie said, and the tension in the room lessened a bit as shaky chuckles rode around the circle. ''Maybe we all do.''

Safe sex, in Millie's vernacular, was jokingly considered to be a good novel with lots of steamy romance.

There was little talk after that point in the meeting. One more person took advantage of the open pitch to discuss his ex-wife's remarriage, but he didn't talk for long, and the meeting ended on a melancholy note.

Cynthia drove home under a starry sky, not certain whether she felt better or not now that she had given voice to the confused feelings which had been rumbling inside of her.

Beth was staying at her grandmother's tonight, and the house was dark when Cynthia arrived. Gwen, Franklin and the girls had left for Portland, and Lane had moved into Lea's.

Cynthia let herself into the house, hung up her coat and scarf and trudged into the kitchen to make a cup of tea. She knew now what the phrase *bone weary* meant. She felt a tiredness that seemed to penetrate her soul. The house was so quiet. This is what it would be like in the years when Beth was grown and living on her own. Cynthia would walk into a house that was quiet and dark. She would turn on the lights, but the silence would remain.

It'll be worse when I'm older, she thought morosely.

In the years to come, she would come home and turn on the television just to hear some sound. To keep herself occupied, she'd find a hobby, like using seashells to make decorative mirrors for Beth's apartment. She would buy a hot-glue gun and make people presents they would sell at garage sales.

And soon the little creaks and whispers of the house as it settled would sound loud to her frail, lonely ears. Living alone in the house, she would become frightened by the possibility of burglars, and she would buy a little canister of tear gas and maybe a small dog that would bark at strange sounds and antagonize neighbors. The dog's incessant yelping would alienate the few friends she had over, and soon those friends would stop coming. Then she'd have to get one of those voice-activated alarms in case she fell down while she was alone and couldn't get up....

Pulling a cup and a tea bag down from a shelf, Cynthia trudged over to the sink to fill a pan with water. At her age, she thought, she should probably be using distilled water, but since all she had was tap— A light beyond the kitchen window caught her eye. She dropped the pan into the sink and turned off the tap. The kitchen window overlooked her backyard. Good Lord, what if there really were burglars out there? She saw another flash of light and leaned over the sink to peer out the window. Burglars with flashlights!

Cynthia squirmed. Hundreds of tiny little flashlights.

She frowned and moved quickly to the door that led to the yard. There was a piece of lined notebook paper upon which Beth had scrawled, ''Merry Christmas, Mom. I love you.'' And underneath that, in Lane's neat hand: ''Merry Christmas, Cyn.''

She opened the door and took one step outside. The sky was black, the air was cold...and every tree

in her yard was decorated with lights, glowing white
lights that blinked ever so slowly. Red ribbons tied
into bows clung to the branches. And glass angels
hung from each bow, suspended with string. The
lights nestled in the branches made the glass angels
glow.

And in the center of the yard, her small plum tree
stood proudly, draped uniquely with tinsel that hung
to the ground. The long, thin threads of gold shim-
mered like hair.

She took another step outside and that's when she
saw at the base of the plum tree a sign which read,
"Cousin It, the second."

Cynthia walked back into the house, closed the
door and burst into tears. She'd never felt less alone
in her whole life.

She awoke the next morning to find that it had
snowed lightly overnight. She looked out her bedroom window and saw that the layer of white made
the trees in her yard look even more magical. Thin
rays of sunshine were poking through the clouds.
They touched the icy particles in the snow and reflected off the glass angels on the trees. The whole
yard seemed to glisten.

It had been cold last night, and Cynthia had slept
in a strawberry-colored sweatshirt and pants, and
bright mustard-colored socks, the toes of which were
flopping loosely against the floor.

She shivered, turning away from the window. Her
head ached and her neck felt sore, like she'd slept
in the wrong position. What she needed was a
shower, then a cup of tea, and then she would ease
into the day. Maybe. There was also the possibility

that she would vegetate under the covers all day, watching CNN.

It was a good plan, but the doorbell rang.

Cynthia debated not answering it. It rang again, more insistently. Running her fingers through her hair she padded downstairs in her socks. The doorbell rang yet again, followed by Beth's call, "Mom, it's me!"

Cynthia opened the door, asking, "What happened to your key?" just as Lane was murmuring to his daughter, "Shh, it's too early to shout."

He looked wonderful—so good, in fact, she instantly forgot her aches and pains.

He was wearing a lightweight wool coat, jeans and a heavy turtleneck in cream. Beth was bundled in her electric-pink down coat. They each held one end of a Christmas tree. Their hair was mussed, and their noses were pink from the cold.

"Hi, Mom! How'd you like your trees? I left my key at Grandma's by mistake."

Cynthia smiled. She gave the only response that was really needed. "I like my trees very much."

Beth beamed. Lane smiled, but he was more reserved today than he had been the night of the home tour.

Cynthia stepped to one side and gestured for them to come in. "Looks like you've brought me another tree."

"Actually, Mom, this one's for me. But you're welcome to help us decorate it."

Beth lugged her end of the tree into the house, and Lane did grin then at his daughter's polite brand of cheekiness. They carried the tree to a corner of the living room, and Lane balanced it on its trunk.

"I'm sorry we barged in without calling first, Cyn. Did we wake you up?"

Becoming acutely aware of her just-up state, Cynthia plucked self-consciously at her sweatshirt. She was braless, but with her build no one would notice unless she did jumping jacks.

"What time is it?" she asked.

Lane looked at his watch. "Five after nine. We wanted to get the tree early. The weather report says more snow."

"Oh." She pushed at her mussed hair and headed for the stairs. "Well, I'm going to go wash up."

"Sure. Cyn—"

She turned at the bottom step.

"I'm glad you liked the trees." Lane watched her walk up the stairs, yellow socks flapping. He turned to his daughter. "Why don't you get the stand? It's on the back seat of the car."

Lane exhaled a long, heavy breath as Beth ran out the door. He'd half expected to find Alan here this morning. Yesterday afternoon, Cynthia had said she had plans last night and couldn't join them for a movie. He and Beth had decided to decorate the yard instead, and he was glad they'd been able to complete the surprise and create Cousin It before she got home. Still, by the end of the evening, he'd been torturing himself with visions of Cynthia and Alan together.

He thought of her floppy yellow socks and smiled. She didn't look like she'd spent a passionate night with a man. She looked like she'd spent a restless night all alone.

It seemed so natural and so right for her to open the door to him in the morning, bleary from sleep,

smiling at their daughter and wearing baggy sweat-
pants and just a sweatshirt over her bare skin.

She'd never needed a bra, he recalled, though she
had modestly worn one. He remembered her as
small and round and perfect. The skin on her chest
was so fair, fairer than her face. Her small nipples
had looked like pink baby rosebuds until she'd become pregnant. Then their color had deepened. He
had loved watching and marveling over the changes
in her.

She had been so shy about her body and about
the process of pregnancy. He had felt shy about it,
too, at first. His discussions of women's bodies had
previously been limited to all-male conversations
with young men whose interests had not included
what a woman looked like while pregnant.

It would be a completely different experience to
go through the process of pregnancy with Cynthia
now. He would want to be more involved. He would
want to touch her body more, be more aware of how
it felt and what each change meant. He wondered if
she would want him to rub lotion on her stomach.
Her stomach had looked so hard, the skin stretched
so tight; he'd thought perhaps she was in pain, but
for some reason he'd been afraid to ask. Maybe because if she'd said yes, he would have felt so damn
guilty.

He'd never told her how frightened he had been
that something would happen to her while she was
pregnant, some medical problem they wouldn't be
able to solve. He'd even had the irrational fear that
she was too young to be pregnant safely.

He almost laughed at himself now as Beth came
running back into the room with the tree stand. He

started to set it up while Beth ran to get the ornaments.

Had Cynthia ever wanted another child? Had *he*? No…never, he realized, not with another woman. But what about now? God, how he would love to make Cynthia pregnant again.

Don't be an idiot, Lincoln. You haven't even had dinner alone with the woman in over ten years. What makes you think she'd want to have your child again?

Lane struggled with the stand, and Beth came back with the decorations. She made three trips to the closet and brought out three large boxes of the Christmas ornaments she and her mother had collected over the years.

They were midway through the second box when Cynthia came downstairs, looking too young, Lane thought, to be the mother of his almost-thirteen-year-old daughter.

Cynthia was wearing dark blue leggings and a deep blue oversize turtleneck sweater. She wore flat navy half boots.

"I think I'll make some breakfast if you two haven't eaten yet."

"Good, I'm starving," Beth said, trying to decide where to hang a pink rocking horse.

Lane nodded. "Don't go to any trouble, though. We'll go out."

"On Christmas-tree morning?" Cynthia scoffed. "Not possible." She tiled her chin toward their daughter. "She won't leave until every ornament is out of those boxes and hung on the tree. You two keep going. I'm just going make something simple."

She wasn't gone long. Lane was just reaching into the third box when Cynthia returned with muffins she'd heated in the toaster oven, two large glasses of orange juice and three cups of hot chocolate. She placed it all on Captain Ahab, the coffee table.

"Mmm!" Beth temporarily abandoned the tree to sit on the floor by the coffee table and grab one of the muffins while they were warm.

Cynthia laughed. "You'd better get over here if you want breakfast. Aunt Fanny doesn't cook, but she does make great apple muffins, and Beth will eat them all if you don't...."

Cynthia's words trailed off when she turned around to see Lane staring at a particular group of ornaments.

"What are these?" he asked quietly, holding a set of photographs in miniature brown picture frames.

"They're for the tree. You hang them up with ribbon." Beth answered without breaking stride in her chewing. She bounced to her feet as if her legs had springs rather than bones inside of them, and moved to her father's side.

"That's Grandma and Grandpa," she said, pointing with her muffin to a picture of Lea and Milton together. "This is Aunt Fanny, that's Aunt Gwen, there's Mom...." She pointed to each of the miniature frames, identifying all the pictures. She saved the best one for last and smiled hugely.

"This is you," she told her father. "But it's you before I knew you. Mom gave it to me for Christmas when I was five. It's a picture of you on the beach in California. I like this picture because it's summery."

She bounced back over to the coffee table like Tigger in a feeding frenzy and grabbed another muffin.

Lane looked at Cynthia. She was stirring her hot cocoa, blowing into the cup. He willed her to look up at him.

She hadn't been obligated to give their daughter a picture of him. He remembered how angry and distant she'd been at the time of their divorce—and how angry and distant she'd stayed. He doubted that she had enjoyed having a picture of him hanging from her Christmas tree. He had been furious and hurt, too, and he had never, after all, even considered having a picture of her in his house where it would remind him of the pain of their breakup.

He watched her until her gaze lifted, and then he mouthed the words *thank you.*

Her nod was barely perceptible. He ached to move toward her, to hold her and to talk about the divorce. He needed to know if she regretted giving up as bitterly as he did.

Do you ever wonder what would have happened if we'd stayed together, Cyn? Do you remember any of the good times? Or did I leave you with memories you'd rather forget? And what would you say if I asked to hold you now, just for a moment…just because we once said we loved each other?

Cynthia wanted to look away from Lane, but couldn't. No matter what she told herself about wisdom and prudence, her heart wouldn't listen. She hated him for walking away. She loved him for Cousin It and the glass angels and for looking into, rather than through, her…and for making her feel the way no man ever had or, she was beginning to believe, ever would.

Damn you, Lane Lincoln, why did you leave? Why couldn't you understand that I was scared? Why didn't you fight the divorce, or ask us to come to L.A. with you? Do you know how many nights I've wished you were holding me?

"It's snowing!"

Their daughter's glad shout shook their gazes free. Beth jumped to the window, pressing her hands and face to the glass.

The snow was falling in fat, lacy clumps; it looked like the flakes were riding piggyback to the ground. The first snow of the season.

Cynthia smiled and swallowed the tears that were threatening her, and that's when she realized how sore her throat was. Her head still ached, too.

Beth was already shoving her arms in her coat.

"Let's go outside. It's falling hard enough for snowballs!" She looked at both of her parents eagerly.

"You go ahead," Cynthia smiled, knowing that her daughter could engage in a snowball battle for hours. "I think I'm getting a cold, honey, and I don't want to be sick for your birthday. I'm going to go back to bed for a while." She started for the stairs before anyone could try to stop her.

Beth was already pulling her father out the door.

Chapter Eight

An hour later Cynthia was in bed with the covers pulled up to her chin, listening to Lane's deep, beautiful baritone and Beth's joyful soprano as they played in the snow. Cynthia had only intended to take a couple of aspirin and read for a while, but her symptoms were worsening with each passing minute. By the time eleven-thirty rolled around, she had a full-fledged, miserable winter cold.

She'd changed into a fresh pair of sweats and less floppy socks when Beth came up to check on her.

Beth was panting from the cold and the fun. "Mom," she said breathlessly, "Dad wants to know if you— Hey, Mom, are you under there?"

Cynthia dragged the pillow off her head. "I'b here, baby. Don't cub too close. I hab a bad cold."

"Wow, you sound really freaky already. You look really terrible, too."

"Thank you."

"You want some aspirin?"

"I already took sub."

"How about some juice? You look really pale."

"Thank you. No juice."

"You should have something," Beth insisted. "You may be dehydrating already. Your eyes are so tired-looking—"

"Thank you, Beth! I feel better just knowing how awful I look. I'll hab a cup of tea, please." Cynthia had raised her head to deliver her thanks, then dropped it back down again.

Beth smiled at her mother's limp form—adults were such babies when they got sick—and skipped back down the stairs.

Cynthia fell asleep again and missed Beth's return. When she awoke, the orange spice tea on her nightstand was stone cold. There were no sounds in the house and no sounds coming from her yard. As far as she could tell, she was alone.

Alone. And feeling very, very sorry for herself. She had been left alone in the house like a dog while lying in her sickbed.

The more Cynthia thought about it—and she thought of little else over the next twenty minutes— the more sorry for herself and the more unloved she felt. *She* never would have left someone this sick home all by themselves. They didn't even know what she had! Oh, sure, the symptoms *mimicked* a cold....

Feeling feverish and tired and absurdly emotional, she thought of all the diseases that had labored breathing, muscle pains or a headache as their chief symptom. By the time her front door opened and closed, she was convinced that she was dying— alone in her room—of a brain tumor.

She was crying with her head under the pillow to muffle her sobs when Lane came into the room to check on her. She hadn't even heard him come up the stairs.

"Cyn?" Expecting to find her still asleep, Lane was shocked to see her with a pillow hugged tightly over her head, her shoulders heaving.

"Cyn, what is it?" As worried as he was surprised, Lane dropped the packages he was carrying and moved swiftly to the bed to put a hand on her arm.

As yet unaware that there was someone else in the room with her, Cynthia jerked. When she peeked out and saw that it was Lane sitting on her bed, she raised herself up and threw her pillow at him. "How could you!" she sobbed, her face streaked with tears.

Lane caught the first pillow and held up his hand as she threw a second one. "What are you doing?"

Cynthia sat on the bed in her pink sweat suit, her blond hair a mess and her eyes overly bright. She had no more pillows, and she began sobbing in earnest.

"I have an aw-aw-awful disease, and no one was here when I woke u-u-u-up!"

Lane had her in his arms before she had the words out. He held her and rocked with her and murmured into her hair while she cried.

"Sweetheart," he crooned. He didn't try to make sense of her behavior; he simply reassured her. "I checked on you before we left. You were sleeping very peacefully, and you weren't even hot. You don't have an awful disease." He smoothed her hair back from her forehead and touched his lips to the top of her head. "You have a cold...and a little fever now, I think." Cynthia became aware of the hand he had placed at the back of her neck, testing for warmth. Gently, it started massaging. "Your nose isn't even as stuffy now as it was. Beth said you couldn't pronounce your *m*'s before."

She felt his smile against the back of her head, then let him move her as he shifted them on the bed.

"Look next to your lamp, Cynthia. Beth wrote a note so you'd know where we were."

Cynthia opened her puffy eyes and blinked. All she could see was a sheet of lined paper. She couldn't read the writing because her eyes were so blurry with tears. She could, however, see Lane's expression when she lifted her head and looked at him.

His eyes were as gentle as his voice—and as patient. He had a soft, genuine smile on his face, a smile intended to encourage rather than to tease. The message in his eyes and the expression on his face said that he would sit there all day if he had to, reassuring her that she was fine—that everything, in fact, was fine.

Cynthia burst into tears again. "I'm sorry I threw the pillows at you." She sobbed into his chest.

"Shhh, it's all right, Cyn." Lane smoothed her hair again. "It can't be the first time you've wanted to throw something at me."

"No." Cynthia hiccuped. "But I never did it before."

Lane laughed. "Well, you must be feeling better, then."

Cynthia drew away and wiped the back of her

wrist across her cheeks and under her eyes. She reached for a tissue. "Where's Beth?"

"She's in the kitchen putting away groceries and heating some soup for you." He gently brushed a strand of hair off her cheek. Suddenly Lane and Cynthia became acutely aware that they were sitting on the same bed. Though he was no longer holding her, his hip was still touching her thigh.

"Knock-knock," Beth chirped, standing just outside the doorway.

"Who's there?" Lane asked unnecessarily while Cynthia grabbed a tissue to wipe her eyes.

"Beth," their daughter answered, her eyes twinkling at the sight of her mother and father sitting together on the bed.

"Beth who?"

"Beth you can't gueth what I made."

Cynthia's laugh sounded like a gurgle as she blew her nose delicately.

Lane stood up to make room for the tray their daughter was carrying.

"That doesn't look like just soup," he said, and immediately Beth noted the praise and the glimmer of pride in his eyes. She'd noticed it there often lately.

"It isn't," she answered, carefully balancing the tray as she placed it across her mother's lap. "It's soup *and* cheese toast *and* a peanut-butter apple."

Cynthia looked down at the tray and smiled. "It looks beautiful, sweetheart." She picked up her spoon and swirled it through the soup. "Chicken with stars."

It was the soup Beth insisted on when she had a cold. Cynthia glanced at Lane. Their eyes locked in a silent communication. *She's growing up, this little girl of ours. Suddenly she's taking care of us.*

"You didn't start the party without me, did you?" Beth asked, glancing around the room.

"Absolutely not," Lane said, crossing to the door to pick up the large bag he had deposited there earlier.

Cynthia tasted the soup. "What party?"

"The I-have-a-cold— What is it, Dad?"

Lane brought the sack to the bed. "It's an I - have - a - cold - but - would - rather - be - out - making - snowmen - so - somebody - cheer - me - up party."

"Snow*people,*" Beth corrected him.

"Right. Sorry." He upended the bag.

Cynthia's eyes widened like a child's at the sight of packages in several different shapes and sizes and all wrapped—haphazardly, to be sure—in bright Christmas paper.

She looked up, questioningly. In Lane's hands, she saw a miniature Christmas tree, no more than six inches high and decorated with miniature candy canes and a red ribbon strung through the branches.

"The lady can't go out to enjoy the winter," he said, removing the cup of cold tea from her nightstand and replacing it with the tree, "so we bring the winter to the lady."

With Cynthia's permission, Beth started unwrapping presents. She knew what was in them, of course, having wrapped the majority of them herself, but the mere act of opening presents this close to Christmas gave her a heady I-shouldn't-be-doing-this thrill.

The first thing she opened was a box of tissues, the extra soft kind with moisturizers, so Cynthia's nose wouldn't get sore. The next gift was smaller—three little boxes of throat lozenges in cherry, honey lemon and extra strength menthol.

With the necessities out of the way, Beth moved on to the more eclectic gifts. There was a box of small paper cups and a jug of pure maple syrup, so they could make real snow cones later if the snow kept falling.

There were tiny plastic sled earrings which Lane had picked out at the drugstore, and a tube of "winter-red" lipstick—Beth's choice, a shade that would make Cynthia look like the bride of Frankenstein.

Then Beth unwrapped a box of graham crackers and a can of white cake frosting.

"What's that for?" Cynthia laughed, pointing to the frosting.

Lane was leaning against a low dresser, watching Cynthia's enjoyment and amusement, and loving it. "The icing is for the graham crackers, of course," he said happily, watching her nose wrinkle.

"That's disgusting."

"No it isn't. It's the best way to take your mind off a cold. By the time you've had one- or two-dozen frosted honey grahams, all you can think about is your stomach."

Cynthia laughed, imploring her daughter to slow down as she tore into the box of graham crackers and snapped open the lid of the frosting.

"Just don't plan on eating too many of those," Cynthia warned. "I don't want to have to think about *your* stomachs all afternoon."

Beth brought out another package, and Lane slipped from the room. Cynthia watched him leave and tried hard not to call him back or question his destination. She'd had no idea—never would have guessed—that she could be so comfortable with him in her bedroom.

She turned her attention to the new package Beth was unwrapping, surprised to see three videos: *Christmas in Connecticut, Miracle on 34th Street* and *Swamp Thing*. Lane returned, carrying her VCR from downstairs, and placed it on the dresser. Beth started spreading frosting on graham crackers and Lane left again, returning a few moments later with the little portable TV she had in the den.

While he hooked everything up, Beth covered some of the highlights of *Swamp Thing*, and Cynthia wondered what her daughter and Lane were going to do this afternoon while she was watching a movie marathon.

The answer was clear when Lane took the tray from her lap and cleared the bed of presents. Beth brought in two more pillows from her room. This was not a movie marathon for one; the content of *Swamp Thing* notwithstanding, they were about to have a family film festival.

Beth stretched out at the foot of the bed. Lane fluffed a pillow and sat with his back against the headboard. They both laughingly disregarded Cynthia's plea to disinfect the room with spray so they wouldn't get sick. As the first film got underway, Beth, Lane and Cynthia each found themselves thinking, *so, this is what it's like to be a family.*

It stopped snowing sometime between *Swamp Thing* and *Christmas in Connecticut*. Beth was growing restless and decided to check on her snow-people before it was completely dark outside.

Lane popped in the Barbara Stanwyck film and returned to sit on the bed.

"You've kept me company all day. You must be getting restless, too," Cynthia told him, trying to absolve him of the responsibility of baby-sitting her.

Lane looked at her with a frown. "Have I given you the impression that I'm restless, Cyn?"

"No...."

"That I'm bored?"

"No, but—"

"That I would rather be somewhere else?"

"No." Cynthia shook her head. "But really, a hundred and twenty-eight minutes of *Swamp Thing* and a sneezing woman? Not exactly the most stimulating afternoon."

"To the contrary, I've always found being stretched out next to you on a bed *extremely* stimulating."

Lane reached his left hand toward Cynthia's arm. He caught a fold of her pink sweat suit between the knuckles of his index and middle fingers, rubbing the soft material without touching her arm. Cynthia felt the sweatshirt pull gently against her forearm. She realized then that she wanted to feel his fingers touch her, even through the material of her sweatshirt.

He had created—in his own unique way—another day that would stand out in her memory from all the days she had spent without him.

Sitting next to him on her queen-size bed, she recalled the very first time she had shared a bed with Lane Lincoln. She had been nervous; he had been eager. She had insisted that he shut off the lights; he had asked her quietly not to pull the sheets up to her neck. Together they had entered a world that had felt brand-new and mysterious to them, a world in which the physical merged with the spiritual and two souls came home.

Now she thought of him touching her again, and for the first time in a long, long time no arguments rose to her mind to reproach her.

Her eyes were on his fingers, and his fingers were still on her shirt. When she felt the tug of the material more insistently this time, she looked up at him.

Lane hadn't moved an inch. He was still sitting with his back straight against her headboard. It seemed that only his fingers had moved.

She gazed at him in question, then realized that he was giving her a silent message...an invitation to come closer. He was leaving the acceptance or refusal completely up to her.

She accepted. Without knowing why—or what had changed to make her suddenly feel that it was the right thing to do—she leaned toward him that first, tentative inch.

Her eyes closed as he moved toward her the rest of the way. She felt the warmth of his body as he came closer, and then...magic.

Her sense of touch seemed to be wholly concentrated in her lips...by the sides of her mouth...on her chin.... There was no feeling anywhere but on the parts of her face that his face touched. His skin was soft and hot beneath a fine shadow of whiskers. His mouth was warm and soft and firm. It moved gently over hers, asking questions, waiting for answers. *Do you like this...and this...? Do you want more? Do you want me as much as I want you?*

He held back, making her hungry while he waited for her responses. And respond she did: *Yes... yes... yes... and yes.* Cynthia drowned in sensations she hadn't felt for ten years. Even her persistent common sense didn't have the gall to tell her she had to stop.

Only when Lane pulled away did total awareness and some sanity return.

"How do you feel?" Lane's murmur was low, his voice thick.

Cynthia realized that he was referring to her health and belatedly remembered that she was contagious.

Her hand flew to her mouth in dismay. "You're going to catch it."

Lane smiled and shrugged. "Then you'll take care of *me*." He reached for her hand and drew it toward him. "Isn't that what people do for each other?"

Cynthia's face grew red. Almost involuntarily her hand inched away from his. She didn't have to say a word. The sadness in the expression she couldn't hide said it all: *Families take care of each other. Husbands and wives do. We're ex-husband and wife. What's that? Something less than strangers.*

Lane watched her, and his expression changed, too. He became pensive. The reality of their situation—the mutual disappointments and the pain from the past—wasn't easily ignored. For either of them.

His attention strayed for a moment to the video, which was still running in the VCR. Barbara Stanwyck was bemoaning her lack of domestic expertise. Lane gave a slight, almost imperceptible shake of his head. Such a simple film; such a simple life. Could they possibly get there from here? He looked again at Cynthia, took a breath and decided to begin at the beginning.

"What we had was good once, Cynthia." His tone told her he would brook no argument on this one point, at least. "We've never talked about the divorce. Even while we were going through it. I assume you had your support systems, and I know I complained to anyone who would listen to me then. But we never discussed the divorce with each other. That was an oversight, don't you think?"

Cynthia didn't miss the irony in his words, or the fact that there was no humor in his inflection, and though the gentleness remained there was a determination in his steady gaze. She saw an openness, too, in his expression, one that she'd never seen before. Missing were the glib twinkle and the cocky confidence.

To each of them, the other person's truest feelings had always been a mystery. Now they would see what could be gained by telling the truth.

Cynthia's hand was lying on the blanket. Lane looked down and once again covered her fingers with his own—but hesitantly this time. It was the first tentative move she had ever seen him make. And as she looked at his downturned face and his slight frown, she knew it was time. Fifteen years ago, she had given this man her heart; now it was time to *open* it to him.

Instead of waiting for Lane to begin, Cynthia started speaking. Sitting on her bed, with her fingers under his and the snow falling again outside, she spoke first of her father and mother and of her years-old determination not to put her children through similar strife. Then she told him about the conversation she'd heard between her parents the night her mother accused her father of not needing his family. She admitted the fear she had harbored deep inside her from that moment on, the fear that she was somehow inadequate, the fear that her father would leave and never come back. And then she admitted the fear she had when Lane had left for L.A.

Lane was holding her hand more tightly now. His voice was thick when he spoke. "It was only supposed to be for a little while, Cyn, I told you that—"

"You made the decision without even discussing it with me!" Cynthia allowed the pain and anger to come through as though the incident had just happened. She remembered suddenly the coolness with which she had discussed it all those years ago, and she vowed to let him see her feelings this time.

Calmly but firmly, she pulled her fingers from his. "Even if it was only supposed to be for a *weekend*, you should have talked to me. I was your wife. We had a little baby, and sometimes I was afraid...." She gave a little laugh. "*Most* of the time I was afraid of the life we were living—no money, big dreams, no stability—and I was afraid that if I complained too much—" here she looked away from him "—you'd get angry or bored...and would want to leave. The possibility that I could do something to drive you away—that scared me more than anything."

"And then I did leave," he finished quietly.

She nodded. "But I'm not blaming you for fulfilling my prophesy. I should have told you how I felt. I should have told you that I needed you. It might not have changed anything—" she shrugged "—but it was so much easier to blame you, to decide that you were just like my father, and that I'd married the wrong man." She smiled wryly. "Then I could give *you* the ultimate rejection before you gave it to me."

"The 'ultimate rejection' being wanting out of the relationship?"

"Yes. To me, the ultimate rejection was somebody not loving me enough to stay."

Lane stood up and walked—paced, actually—to the window. He was so filled with emotion that he couldn't put his finger on precisely what he was feeling. He did recognize, however, burning frustration and anger for all the lost years.

He turned to Cynthia and, like her, allowed his feelings to flood his expression. "I understand your fears, Cynthia, but I did come back. I never said or indicated in any way that I wanted a damned divorce."

"No," Cynthia returned, "you wanted it all. A career in California, a family to come back to occasionally." She rushed ahead when he was about to protest. "You came back for *visits,* Lane. You'd bring a gift for Beth, a little something for me, but you weren't there when she said her first word, or when she had croup...or when I needed a husband."

Lane said nothing for a while. He stared out the window at the snowpeople he and Beth had made earlier. One was dressed like W. C. Fields and the other like Mae West.

You weren't there.... She'd hit the nail on the head with that one. He'd had fears, too, and that was the biggest—that his family would need him, and he wouldn't be there.

He had known, too, how much she had hated his leaving. He'd known and he'd left, anyway.

He looked at Cynthia, who was sitting on the bed with her delicate hands in her lap. He'd always loved her hands. She was gazing up at him expectantly, waiting for him to say something, to explain why he had gone to L.A. and left her in Oregon.

He moved both hands through his hair. His face was filled with pain. "I never stopped loving you, Cynthia. I never stopped wanting you and Beth to be my family."

She had waited more than half her adult life to hear those words. "Why didn't you fight the divorce?" she asked in a small, choked voice. "You never tried to stop it. I remember you just threw the papers on the floor and said, 'The hell with it.'"

So, that's how she remembers it, Lane thought, knowing that his version of that day was more damning.

He remembered returning to Oregon with the divorce papers in hand. His rage had been towering, palpable. He'd asked if she was serious, if she truly meant to break up their family. He would never forget—no matter how hard he tried—the disbelief and the anger in her eyes as she answered, "What family?" Nor would he forget the bitter twist she had put on the word *family.*

Most clearly and painfully of all, though, he remembered his response. He had thrown the papers on the floor, grabbed her by the arms, and had virtually growled in her stricken face, "To hell with it, then. And to hell with you. I just want my daughter."

Apologize now, he told himself fiercely. *Tell her*

you remember, and tell her you never meant a word of it.

Her green eyes were filled with sadness and something more poignant—hope. It was a look he hadn't dared dream he'd ever see in Cynthia's eyes again. He struggled for the words that would explain everything.

He took her hands and raised them to his lips. "I'm sorry," he murmured, "I'm sorry. You were honest with me, Cyn, and I want to be honest with you."

He shook his head.

What could he tell her? He'd asked himself the same question thousands of times over the years, unable to figure out the answer, yet knowing he'd give anything to go back and do it all over differently. What could he say that would make any sense when he didn't fully understand his past actions himself? He hadn't fought the divorce. He hadn't wanted it and yet he hadn't truly fought it. He'd been hurt and shocked by her rejection. It was hard to admit it, but maybe he simply hadn't had the courage to fight her when it seemed so clear that she no longer believed in their love—or in *him*.

He wanted to give her the answers she needed. He still couldn't unravel the past entirely, much less change it. Lane was banking on the future now, and on the hope that with a little luck and lots of courage he could convince this woman to believe in their love again. This time when he asked her to be his wife, he wanted to give her a hundred and one good reasons for believing it would last forever.

He looked her squarely in the eye and knew that

from now on he would speak nothing but the truth to this woman, no more and no less.

He turned her hand over in his, smoothing her palm with his thumb. "After Beth's birthday on Saturday, I'm flying to Los Angeles for a week." He held tightly to her hand when she tried to pull away. "One week, that's all," he told her firmly. "When I come back, Cyn, I'm going to ask you to be my wife. And this time I'm going to give you every reason to believe that we're going to last forever."

He squeezed her fingers and shook his head when she opened her mouth. "Don't say anything right now. Please...trust me. Don't give me all the reasons why it won't work, because in ten days I'm going to be back here giving you all the reasons why it will. For now, though..."

His hand drifted up to the nape of her neck. His thumb caressed the spot behind her ear.

"For now, here's the best reason of all."

He pulled her in, and his kiss was more thorough this time, more passionate. And so convincing.

When he drew back, he was still less than a whisper away. "I love you. We're even for now, Cyn. You told me how you used to feel, and I'm telling you how I feel right now. In ten days, we change roles."

It was a warning to be ready...and a promise she prayed he would keep.

Chapter Nine

Beth swore it was the best birthday she'd ever had. Her eyes shone with pleasure and thanks.

The party was simple enough. Family and Beth's friends gathered in Cynthia's home. Tom and Theresa Moreau of Theresa's Cantina in Ashland supplied the food. They recruited Lane to help in the kitchen, and the three of them sang selections from *West Side Story*—their version of cantina music—while they rolled Theresa's famous burritos. They stuffed each gargantuan tortilla with rice, beans, guacamole, lettuce, sour cream, salsa, cheese and each person's choice of chicken, beef, pork or steamed veggies. Only Lane and Gwen chose chicken, beef, pork *and* steamed veggies.

Aunt Fanny poured root beer and offered to teach three thirteen-year-old girls how to apply eye makeup just like hers. Cynthia cringed.

Gwen ate...and ate...and insisted that Franklin buy several quarts of Theresa's avocado salad dressing and an ice chest so she could take the dressing to L.A.

As he did in his restaurant, Tom tried to arrange some sort of harmony on the "Happy birthday, dear Be-e-eth," but was unsuccessful. Milton and Lea cut cake and scooped ice cream and clapped the loudest when Beth blew out all her candles on one try. No one had to ask what she'd wished for. Her gaze lifted to find her parents when the candles were snuffed, and she beamed. She wanted more birthdays like this one.

Late that night Cynthia sat on the couch by herself and privately agreed with her daughter. Today they had shared family, community and the joy of making a child's simple dream—having all of her family in the same room on her birthday—come true. It had been a good, good day.

Lane's surprise gift to Beth had been two plump, healthy Lab-mix puppies. Lane had picked the dogs up from the Jackson County animal shelter, and Beth and her friends had been beside themselves.

Mario and Luigi—the puppy brothers were named after Beth's favorite video game—were currently sleeping off their big day. Mario was on the floor by the coffee table, and Luigi was sleeping on Cynthia's lap, lying on his back with his legs spread like a dead frog's. His warm, pink puppy belly rose and fell under her hand.

The rest of the house was silent now, and empty.

Franklin had taken Lane to the airport. Beth and her cousins had gone along for the ride. A glance at the clock told Cynthia that Lane was already on his way back to L.A., and with that knowledge all of Oregon started to seem empty.

She had it bad.

Together with Beth, she and Lane had enjoyed a wonderful week since the day of her "I-have-a-cold" party. Cynthia had avoided R.A. meetings, and her agent, and any reminders of "real" life. They'd just been together, as a family. Every glance and touch between herself and Lane had only revived the best memories of their past, and made her imagine him ever-present in her future.

Luigi started to dream, his black nose twitching and his little paws flapping as he chased something in his sleep. She rubbed his tummy and smiled as he quieted and bared his teeth in a puppy grin.

It had been so wonderful to watch Beth with her friends today. They were young ladies who had turned into squealing girls again at the sight of a puppy. In that way, the puppies had been a gift for Cynthia, as well. Opportunities to see her daughter as a child were dwindling fast as Beth took her last eager steps toward young womanhood.

It was rewarding and joyous to watch her grow and change. But sometimes Cynthia despaired of ever holding another baby in her arms. Of filling the house with childish squeals again and the scent of baby powder. Or of filling her arms with the wondrous softness of baby skin and the unselfconscious need of a child.

Cynthia brushed the backs of her fingers up Luigi's furred chest and back down. She closed her eyes as the unbidden images she'd denied herself for years came rushing in unchecked now—the small room off her own dressed as a nursery; Lane holding a baby high over his head, his strong neck arched, his head tilted back, and both he and the baby grinning and laughing; she, dressed in a robe, bringing Lane coffee as he worked on a script; and later, she without her robe, at long last holding more in that bed of hers than just a pillow.

He'd promised her truth and had implied a new beginning. She'd promised to trust. She hoped they could both keep their word.

The doorbell rang, and Cynthia gently moved Luigi off her lap. She glanced at Mario, who was also sleeping soundly. Watchpuppies they were not.

When Cynthia saw Gwen through the peephole, she pulled the door open without delay. "What are you doing here?"

"Hi, sis, I'm fine. How are you?" Gwen walked in, rubbing her gloved hands together.

Cynthia closed the door and followed her sister to the couch. "You were just here, I know how you are. You should be home, resting."

Gwen smiled at Mario and sat down next to Luigi. "Zeke would love these two. He could be a surrogate daddy at last." She sighed heavily and shrugged out of her coat. "You keep it nice and warm in here. I like this house."

Cynthia saw the tiredness and the stress around her sister's pretty eyes. "Gwen, it is ten-thirty at night. You would never put on shoes at ten-thirty if you didn't have to. Now tell me what's going on."

She took a seat on a plaid wing-back chair as she waited for Gwen to begin.

Gwen toyed with her wedding ring. "I have something to tell you, and I didn't want to do it over the phone."

"Oh, my God, the car!" Cynthia leapt to her feet. "There was an accident!"

Gwen looked up at her, mouth open, brows lowered. "No there wasn't."

"The plane. Oh, my God, not the plane...." Cynthia whispered, her hands clenched against her stomach.

"Have you always been such a worrier? The plane's fine, I'm sure." Gwen checked her watch. "Just took off fifteen minutes ago. I wanted to talk to you before Franklin and the girls got back." She turned her head to the side and eyed her sister askance. "Sit down, will you? You're making me nervous."

Cynthia complied, and Gwen tucked her hair behind her ears. "I got a phone call a little over an hour ago...." Her voice trailed off, and she played with the face of her wristwatch.

"Who called?"

Gwen's head came up; she looked her sister square in the eye. "Dad."

"Dad." Cynthia's voice was too breathy to be a croak, too dry to be a whisper. She crossed one leg over the other, pressing thigh to thigh to suppress the shivers that were traveling through her body.

She sat back in the chair and crossed her arms, as well. When she spoke, her voice was flat and nonchalant. "Whose dad is that?"

Gwen expelled the breath she'd been holding. "You know whose dad, Cynthia." She slapped one palm onto the seat cushion. Luigi's head came up briefly, then dropped woozily down again. "Dammit," Gwen swore, "I knew you were going to do this. That's why I wanted to tell you in person, so I could see beneath the surface. You're shaky, aren't you? I was, too. I started shaking right away, as soon as I heard his voice—like I was freezing cold. It's a nervous reaction. Backed-up emotions. I asked the counselor at Franklin's school about it, because I noticed that it happens to you and me when we're nervous.''

''What else did you ask the counselor?'' Cynthia's voice was soft, her eyes sharp.

Gwen met her head-on. ''I asked her to help me learn how to forgive him.''

Cynthia nodded almost imperceptibly. ''Did you also ask how damaging it might be if you let him walk into your life again, into your children's lives, playing the Pied Piper and then disappearing again?''

''It didn't come up. I never thought I'd see him again.''

''Bingo.''

Gwen leaned forward as far as she could in her condition. ''But he *did* come back…he did call, Cynthia. Those phone calls I told you about, when I would pick up the phone and there was nobody on the other line? That was him. He was trying to work up the nerve to say hello.''

Gwen's voice softened and her eyes filled on her last word.

Cynthia brought one hand up to her temple and shook her head. ''Great. He was too frightened back then to say goodbye to his wife and children. He was too frightened to let us know whether he was alive or dead. Now he's too frightened to say hello.'' She looked at her sister. ''I can see you've already forgiven him. What are you here for, Gwen—my blessing to invite him to Christmas dinner?''

Gwen struggled up from the couch, reaching back for her coat. ''I don't need your blessing for that, Cynthia. I certainly wouldn't expect it. Since when have you ever forgiven anybody who transgressed your personal standards for human behavior?''

She jammed her arms into the coat as Cynthia rose from her chair. ''That is not fair,'' Cynthia gasped.

Gwen's hands flapped at her sides. She shook her head and walked to the door. ''Maybe it isn't fair.'' She faced the front door with her hand on the knob. ''But I feel like I'm betraying you somehow by deciding to see him.'' She turned. ''I used to think you were weird, working for hours on a stupid card trick, following him around everywhere.'' She smiled and shrugged. ''I liked being in the kitchen, baking cakes with Mom. Maybe you loved him more than I did then. But he's my father, too, and I'm not going to turn my back on that without giving it a fighting chance.''

She opened the door, paused and said one last thing. ''He's staying at the Motel 6 in Medford.''

When Gwen shut the door behind her, Cynthia moved to the window and pushed the drapes aside to watch her sister walk to the car. She watched Gwen get in and watched the taillights disappear down the dark block. She had no idea how long she stood there, the drapes lying like a shawl across her shoulder and back, before she finally noticed the snow wafting down like white flower petals tossed from a balcony.

Gwen didn't know all of it, Cynthia thought, not

sure if she was excusing her sister or excusing herself. Gwen hadn't heard the fight between their parents that one awful night, and Cynthia had never told her about it.

Gwen was right about one thing: Cynthia had shadowed their father wherever she could.

It was the magic, she thought, placing the palm of one hand against the window and watching the warmth from her hand fog the cold glass. *I just couldn't resist the magic.*

Henry couldn't have survived without elevating each day to a special occasion. He had been hopelessly, foolishly romantic.

Briefly, Cynthia allowed herself to wonder what he looked like now. Did he still have that way of hitching the waist of his trousers with his wrists when he was enthusiastic about something? Did he still get that faraway look in his eyes when he read the newspaper?

"What are you thinking about, Daddy?"

"About all the places we'll see someday, Cinnamon Girl."

Cynthia watched the flakes falling outside her window and rubbed her hand on the glass.

"Where do snowflakes come from, Daddy?"

She bent her forehead to the glass.

"It's the angels sending us Christmas cards...."

Cynthia stayed for a moment exactly as she was. She closed her eyes.

"Oh, Daddy, why couldn't *you* have sent us a Christmas card?"

Her breath was warm against the windowpane, but the rest of her stayed cold.

The difference one note would have made during

the lonely years. Just one note to say he hadn't forgotten them…or an address where Cynthia could have written to tell him she'd gotten her braces off, or any of the hundred other things she'd wanted to share with him over the years.

She felt the tears welling inside her. She let them fall for as long as she dared, dropping the curtains and drying her eyes before Beth arrived. She took Mario and Luigi to the kitchen to tuck them in for the night. She moved stiffly, automatically, and as hard as she tried not to, she couldn't help but compare her father's inability to communicate all those years ago with Lane's inability—or unwillingness—to communicate the other night.

"Trust me," he'd asked her.

I'm trying. I want to.

But as she moved through the silent house, willing her heart to stay open, she could feel it slowly, inexorably beginning to close.

Chapter Ten

Lane was sitting in his agent's office on Wilshire Boulevard in Beverly Hills. He was leaning back in a burgundy leather monstrosity of a chair that bounced when sat on—intended, obviously, for people who liked to swivel while they wheeled and dealed.

Cook Russel had been Lane's agent for the past eight years. Cook was, for the first time in their profitable association, on the verge of resigning. He leaned forward over his desk, tapped the blotter with his pen and decided to try one more tactic before he gave up on the most successful client he'd ever had.

"You're an ingrate," he accused, one hand tapping the pen, the other drumming impatient fingers. "'I want to direct, Cook,' you said. 'I want more control, Cook.'" He spread his hands, palms up. "Isn't that what I'm giving you?"

He pointed the pen at Lane, raising his other hand behind his head as he leaned back in his own swivel chair. He nodded toward the papers on his desk. "That deal is the best we'll get, and it's damn good. You haven't directed yet. I hate to remind you of this, but you're unproven. You start making too many demands now and they'll tell us to take a nice, long walk." His eyebrows rose skyward for added emphasis.

Lane frowned and didn't even bother to hide his irritable glance at his watch. He wanted to finish this and get out of here. Cook's office smelled like too much leather and cologne.

"What's wrong," he asked, "with a location shoot in Oregon?"

"A location shoot in Oregon I can get you." Cook lunged forward again, unable to stay in one position for very long. "But a year long delay while you take care of a personal matter? No one will go for that." He ran both hands over his face. "I don't understand you. I got you just what you've been asking me for the past two years, and now when we've got everything lined up—the money, the names—you start hedging! What is so important that you have to do it right now, for God's sake?"

He shook his head, rested his elbows on the desk and clasped his hands. He pursed his lips against his knuckles. "Do you have some kind of…problem, Lane? Listen, if you need somewhere to dry out, try Betty Ford's place. Six weeks—you're in and you're out. We could keep it quiet. You might even make some good contacts." He spoke the last to himself and rolled his chair forward so he could flip through his address book.

Lane shot forward so fast, the chair almost dumped him onto the Berber carpeting. "I do not need to go to a clinic!" he thundered. "I need to go to Oregon to get my wife back."

Cook blinked twice. "Wife? When the hell did you get married?"

Lane stood and paced to the window that overlooked Wilshire Boulevard. He was starting to hate the noise, the hustle, the pollution. It left no room to think.

"You're talking about the first one, aren't you?" Cook concluded. "The one who wrote that book?"

Lane's teeth ground together and his jaw tensed. He had finally read "that book," had understood the heroine's need to intellectualize the process of falling in love. If she could intellectualize it, she could control it. He did not, however, appreciate the fact that Susan and Theodore went their separate ways in the end.

When he sensed that Cook was waiting for an answer, he turned and almost growled at the man who had helped him build his career. "They call it a *private* life for a reason, Cook."

"Yeah. And they call me an agent because I represent you. I want to know if I'm representing a lunatic."

There was a brief standoff until Cook sighed and relented. "Hey, Lane, we're friends, too, right? I worked on this deal and told everyone your availability was a given whenever they set the date. I'll go back to them and tell them you can't do it until next summer—"

"Fall."

For just a moment Cook looked like he would argue, but then he agreed. "Fall. And I'll tell them you'll only shoot in Oregon. But give me a reason, buddy. Tell me something I can understand, because you may be walking away from the best offer I'll ever swing for you."

Here it is, Lane thought, *the choice.* It wasn't the first time he'd had to make it.

He looked at Cook, opened his mouth for a glib but final reply, and then realized that he respected Cook Russel too much to hide behind flippancy.

Nine years ago, with no family and no career at all, Lane had pounded on Cook's door, figuratively speaking. He'd had a need to succeed that had been burning, raw and all-consuming. Cook had believed in him and had guided his career to heights he had only dreamt of before. They had both looked forward to this first directing job with great relish. And Cook had indisputably worked hard to secure it. They'd put together a good package and had lined up strong actors. He couldn't risk it all without telling Cook why.

And so, all the fears and all the confusion Lane wrestled with regarding his marriage and its early failure were brought to light in Cook Russel's office. As Lane spoke, prompted by respectful questions from Cook, he began to put together the pieces of the puzzle.

"My sister was a figure skater." His voice rolled through the room as he gazed out at Wilshire Boulevard. "She was shooting for the junior regional championship. My mother drove her to the rink every morning to practice. One Saturday close to the skate finals, my father decided to go, too." Lane smiled. "I remember he tried to make me go with them, promised me a big breakfast out. But I was eight and a helluva lot more interested in sleep than getting up at four to drive to an ice rink.

"It was winter and the first ice of the season was on the road. Black ice, the kind you can't even see. My father was driving. A van slid into them and they slid into a telephone pole...."

Lane paused a moment, and when he resumed speaking, his voice was matter-of-fact.

"Everything changed after that. I went to Idaho to live with an aunt, but I never got close to her. I just *expected* to lose people after that, I think, and for a long time I kept my distance. I thought there must be some reason, some flaw in me God was angry about." He laughed, but the pain was louder than the amusement. "So I planned a career, a big one, the kind of career that could take the place of a family. The kind of career that could say—" he tilted his head back and raised a fist at the ceiling "—'Look at me. What do You know? I made it. I have something. And You didn't give it to me, so You can't take it away.'"

He lowered his fist and smiled wryly. "The joke was on me, though, I guess, because before I wrote my first script I fell in love."

"When did you meet your wife?"

"Cynthia." Lane supplied the name he'd never mentioned to Cook. "We met in college. I was nuts about her right off the bat—and terrified, which I didn't realize then. I was convinced I'd lose her, one way or another. I think I pulled away long before she did."

"I thought your career broke you up," Cook said, remembering the one other time Lane had mentioned his marriage.

Lane paused a moment, considering carefully before he answered. "That's what I told myself…that and a lot of unflattering things about her loyalty. But you know what I remembered just last week? I never even asked her to come to L.A. with me. I mean *really* asked her. We talked about it, but it was always off in the future—next month, or the month after that."

Cook saw Lane's frown and knew that his client and friend was trying to puzzle out the whys and the wherefores.

"I know *now* why I put it off. I wanted to bring her out here when I was a big success. I didn't want her to see me fail. I thought if she did, I'd lose her. And deep down, I thought I was going to lose her, anyway, like I lost my family."

Both men were silent for a time. Then Cook said, "I assume this means that all of your movies will be set in Oregon now?"

"Or wherever she'll go with me."

The agent nodded. "All right, take your year. And don't worry about me. I'll get by. I can always get a job at Del Taco. I think they have a manager trainee program for ex-Hollywood agents."

Lane grinned, but didn't feel too sorry for his friend. Cook's client list read like the seating chart at the Academy Awards. For Cook there would always be another deal around the corner. He proved it with his next request.

"Just do me one favor, will you? See if she'll sell you the screen rights to her book." He grabbed a pad of paper and started scribbling notes to himself. "No deferments, we take ten percent of the gross, she has script approval…"

*   *   *

In the small wood-paneled den in Cynthia's mother's house, five people were huddled around a nineteen-inch color TV, their eyes glued to the screen.

Aunt Fanny, dressed in a leopard-print bodysuit and filmy blouse, clashed violently with the striped velour of the recliner she was sitting on. Lea, Gwen and Franklin sat side by side on the sofa. Gwen had a huge bowl of cheddar-cheese popcorn perched precariously on what was left of her lap, and Lea's husband, Milton, was standing next to the set, adjusting and readjusting the antennae.

The "Art 'n Barbie" show was about to begin. And Cynthia was going to be on it.

"There's too much red in the picture. Fix it, Milt," Lea directed her husband as she reached for the popcorn bowl.

Gwen grabbed at the bowl like a drowning person clutching at a life preserver. "I'll hold it, Mom. I didn't have much breakfast."

"That's true," Franklin concurred, reaching into the popcorn to secure a meager handful before his delicate wife scarfed it all, lock, stock and kernel. He smiled at his mother-in-law. "That ham steak you gave her couldn't have been more than eight or ten ounces, Lea, and I only left half of my potatoes for her to finish." He leaned over to kiss his wife. "You sure you don't want another Danish, honey, to tide you over till the show starts?"

"Oh, be quiet." Gwen grinned around a mouthful of popcorn. She had the metabolism of a stevedore, so she didn't mind their teasing. She shook her head as she watched her stepfather fumble with the color control.

"Now the TV's green. Cynthia looks lousy in green." She slapped her husband's arm with the back of her hand. "Help Milton, honey."

Franklin unfolded his tall frame and moved to the TV. Gwen watched the picture go from green to red and back again as the appliance-store owner and the science teacher monkeyed with the set.

Gwen wanted Cynthia's skin tones to look like skin tones. She wanted to see the same picture she imagined her father was seeing in his motel room in Medford.

Cynthia had not agreed to visit him, and she and Gwen had ceased to discuss it, but Gwen had told their father about the show. His eyes had turned watery, and a wide, amazed grin had stretched his lined mouth.

"Cynthia on TV? Well, isn't that somethin'," Henry had whispered in awe. "Just isn't that somethin'." He had excitedly declared his intention to watch the show in his motel.

"That's it! Hold it right there!" Gwen stretched out her hand, jostling the popcorn.

"For heaven's sake, leave it alone now—everyone—and sit down." Aunt Fanny had a voice that could melt butter, even when she was feeling testy. She crossed her long legs and readjusted the collection of bangles clinking on her wrist. "Lea, sweetie," she said to her sister, "do you know that they actually make twenty-five-inch television sets now? Ask Milton to get you one for Christmas."

Lea simply smiled. Whenever her elder daughter was on TV, the size of the screen ceased to matter to her. She would have watched the show on a wristwatch. Knowing that Henry would be watching their daughter, as well, made this particular show that much more special.

"This is a good set," Milton asserted, patting the old television like it was man's best friend. "Nice big tubes you can see."

Lea smiled fondly at her second husband.

Henry James had been all wrong for her. He was a dreamer. He loved ideas and spontaneity and change. She was—and always would be—a realist, she liked solid things, like pasts and presents and futures that were planned. No, she and Henry had been as wrong for each other as sandals on a duck's feet. They hadn't needed what the other could give. She was only sorry that she had blamed him for what had been a joint failure.

Lea looked at the people in her homely den.

Milton was still extolling the virtues of his aged television. "Yup. This li'l baby's as easy to fix as pancakes on Sunday."

Fanny was rolling her eyes.

Gwen and Franklin were fighting for the popcorn.

Lea enjoyed her family. The only one she worried about now was Cynthia. It seemed strange to worry about a person who was about to be on television for the third time in two months, but the happiness Lea wanted for her elder child couldn't be reaped from a bestseller list.

Sighing, Lea smiled fondly at her husband just as he was about to launch into a comparison of his television versus newer models.

"Sit down now, Milton dear. The show is about to begin."

Cynthia blinked against the brightness of an ungelled light that a technician was pointing her way.

He slipped an amber-colored gel into the frame to soften the glare, and Cynthia's forehead relaxed.

Another day, another interview.

But this was the last one, she swore to herself as she tried to slow the rapid beating of her heart with long, slow breaths. This was just a local cable show she'd rashly agreed to months ago, but her central nervous system couldn't be reasoned with. A camera was a camera, and when they were pointed her way, her anxiety level skyrocketed. Besides, this was an anomaly—a live local cable show.

"'Scuse me, Ms. James, why don't we powder you one last time."

The young makeup artist bent forward with a flat, round container of loose powder and a puff which looked like it had been around since the Golden Days of Hollywood. Hygiene aside, Cynthia could feel perspiration beading along her forehead and upper lip, so she obediently lifted her face.

The makeup artist smiled, sending the tiny diamond stud in her nose up a notch.

"These lights are really warm," she said. "I have to powder everybody three or four times."

Cynthia frowned at the powder puff as it dabbed along her upper lip. Hot lights and camera jitters weren't the only culprits responsible for her sweat-a-thon. Yet, there was something different about her stage fright this time. All the other times, she'd been nervous but eager to talk about her book.

But now, for the first time, she had no desire to discuss it.

Since her conversation with Gwen several nights before, Cynthia was little more than a five-foot-seven-inch amalgam of bone, water, flesh and confusion. She and Gwen were back on good terms, though they both avoided the topic of their father. Cynthia wasn't even certain that he was still in town, but try as she might, she could not deny the sense of loss that assailed her every time she thought that he may have disappeared again without her seeing him.

Then there was the fact that Lane hadn't called.

Trust me. His words clanged around in her head.

She wanted to kill him.

She wanted to kiss him.

She wanted him to kiss her the way he had on her bed, using his tongue and his hands until she felt like they were two nascent butterflies—just getting ready to taste the world outside, but for now sharing the same warm cocoon.

"We're at one minute, please."

The production assistant flashed one finger, and the makeup artist gave Cynthia a final dab before moving away.

The host of the show, Barbara Atchity, slid into her chair, picking up the tiny clip-on microphone that was draped over the chair arm. She clipped the mike to the lapel of her blazer and smiled at Cynthia.

"Great book. Just finished it. Men stink." She turned her smile to the camera.

Cynthia gulped.

Music rolled.

"Hello, I'm Barbara Atchity, and you're watching 'Art 'n Barbie.'" Her voice was as smooth as warm honey. "We're focusing on the written word as art today, and I have with me a local author who's climbing the bestseller charts with her pointed ac-count of—'' Barbara's voice dipped dramatically ''—*a marriage gone wrong*. Meet the Southern Or-egonian mother with the razor-sharp pen—Cynthia James. Cynthia, welcome.''

Cynthia gulped again.

On the couch in Lea's den, Milton reached over and patted his wife's hand.

''Cyndi looks good,'' he said. ''I think we got out all of the green.''

Aunt Fanny wagged her head and snorted omi-nously. ''I've seen this show. Barbara Atchity hates men.'' She adjusted one of the crystal earrings that dangled to her shoulder.

The doorbell rang.

''Get that, dear, would you?'' Lea directed her husband absently as Barbara Atchity told Cynthia that her book ''helps women break free of the shack-les love clamps on our nimble female legs.''

They watched the screen as Barbara canted with evangelical zeal, and Cynthia did an inordinate amount of gulping and rapid blinking.

Milton returned to the room just as Barbara At-chity flipped to a premarked page in Cynthia's book.

''In chapter eleven,'' she stated, ''you render Theodore impotent.'' She leaned over her knees like a gossip monger ready to dish. ''Tell me, Cynthia, is it true that Theodore is modeled after your ex-husband?''

''Hey, everybody,'' Milton singsonged in his pleasant voice, ''look who's here.''

Four heads turned.

Lane Lincoln was standing in the doorway. He pulled his gaze from the TV and tried to smile.

Cynthia was starting to perspire heavily again, and she knew it wasn't because of the lights.

She was starting to panic under Barbara Atchity's cross-examination.

"Do you believe men have all the advantages in a marital relationship?"

"Well…"

"How about in an affair?"

"Oh, uh, I don't…"

"In your book you suggest that traditional views of romance should become obsolete."

"Uh, y-yes, but what I meant was—"

"I agree completely!"

Barbara Atchity was driving her like a cowboy drives steer, and Cynthia had the sickening, gummy feeling that slaughter lay just around the bend.

She had no control over this interview because she didn't know what she wanted to say. In the past, it had always seemed convenient—and very good publicity—to let interviewers dwell on the more controversial aspects of the book and on her assertion that romantic notions could be dangerous.

But Cynthia was beginning to believe that there was something far more dangerous than being a slave to passion. Being a slave to *fear* was crippling her.

In the days since Lane had left, she had determinedly thrust aside the desire to trust him. Instead, she thought of her father. She dredged up the old hurt and then cloaked herself in it the way a parent bundles a child against the rain.

And she was miserable.

She missed the anticipation of longing for Lane's return. She missed the exciting thirst that came with letting herself wonder when he would kiss her next.

The refusal to trust, to allow herself to hope, left her feeling like a balloon with all the air let out of it.

She met Barbara Atchity's feverish eyes and took a deep breath before speaking.

"Theodore and Susan's relationship in the book does mirror my relationship with my ex-husband in some ways." It was her first willing admission, and Barbara was rapt. "The pain of..." Cynthia paused, searching for the words, wanting to be accurate, "...of coming to a relationship with scars can be very intense. I had unreal expectations, and I expected Lane, my husband, to make up for past hurts he had no part in. I thought being in love would make my life perfect. I thought I'd never feel bored or hurt or lonely again....

"There's an old saying that your cup of joy can only be as deep as your cup of sorrow. Maybe we can only feel love to the extent that we're willing to risk pain."

Cynthia continued to speak softly and slowly, sidestepping Barbara's thirst for brash, extreme statements. She was hesitant at times, unsure of precisely the point she was trying to make at others, but she got through the show without saying anything she *didn't* want to say, and she felt lighter somehow, and freer. Her uncertainty was more liberating than her rigidity.

She left the studio feeling shaky, but better than she had felt walking in. She was due at a noon R.A.

meeting. She wondered if the women and men there had seen the program and, if so, what their reactions would be.

When she arrived at the meeting place, the converted basement of an old church, it was two minutes to twelve, and Cynthia had to take a seat in the back of the cavernous room.

The group availed itself of a podium and microphone belonging to the church. Both the size of the room and the size of the group made a microphone necessary, but some people shied away from speaking vulnerably into a mike during the open pitch.

The seat next to Cynthia's was vacant, and Cynthia was surprised when Millie Dalton slipped into it.

"Millie, what are you doing at this meeting?" Cynthia whispered to her after a hug. "I thought you hated crowds."

"I do." Millie snapped her gum and shrugged. "But I caught 'Art 'n Barbie.' Made me feel like comin' to a meeting." She crossed her arms over her thin chest and settled comfortably in her seat. "I liked what you had to say, kid. It was honest. Made us seem less militant, you know what I mean? 'Course, next to that bulldozer, Barbie, anyone'd seem moderate."

Cynthia smiled.

The crowd settled and the meeting got underway. First the twelve steps of Romantics Anonymous were recited en masse. Then the day's speaker opened with, "Hi, I'm Judith Anne, compulsive romantic," to which the group responded—again en masse—"Hi, Judith Anne." Judith Anne spoke for half an hour, and then it was time for the open pitch, when anyone who had something to say could step up to the mike.

The first speaker to the podium was a man who announced that he was new to the meetings.

"I saw Cynthia James on television today," he said, speaking comfortably into the microphone. "I was very impressed with everything she had to say."

Millie nudged Cynthia, but Cynthia didn't even feel it. For just an instant all movement, all sound seemed to stop. She felt like her heart had paused and wouldn't beat again until he resumed speaking. She gazed at that face—so serious, so strong—the face of the man she'd loved for so long. She knew that she wouldn't have moved if the building were on fire.

"I don't know if I'm a compulsive romantic," he continued, running his fingertips along the edge of the podium as he frowned, "but I do know that I'm still in love with my ex-wife."

His gaze drifted down to the podium, then lifted again as he continued. "I was very young when we met, but I hadn't said 'I love you' to anyone in a long, long time. When she said it to me, I thought—" he paused, looking for words to match the feelings "—'nothing in your life will ever feel this good... don't blow it.'" He released his breath and the exhalation sounded harsh in the quiet room. He smiled slightly. "As far as fear goes, I'd say falling in love ranks right up there with going to the dentist for the first time."

Nods and chuckles drifted around the room.

"You know how you feel when you watch the

sun set over the ocean? There's always that one perfect moment that's so good you're afraid to look
away because you don't want to miss it, and you're
afraid for the moment to come, because then you
know it'll have to end. Well, that's how I felt with
Cynthia. I knew when she said 'I love you' that she
was my one perfect moment.''

He swallowed, and his voice dropped to a raspy
whisper that sounded hollow and almost mournful
in the echo of the microphone. ''She told me once
that I never fought to save our marriage. She's right.
I was so damn sure it was going to end and that I
was going to lose her that I think…I helped it
along.''

His face grew stormy. His eyes searched for and
found the one person in the room to whom he
wanted to speak. ''All these years, I thought it
would take a miracle to bring us back together again.
But then I saw her, and I knew that the miracle had
already happened. We never stopped caring. It was
there all the time—we just had to be able to see it,
and admit to it. To just believe in it. I know there's
no going back, and it's a tough journey forward…but if we care—a lot—then maybe that's reason enough to try.''

There was silence when he stopped talking. There
were stares when he didn't resume his seat. But
Lane Lincoln knew where he had to begin to reach
his journey's end, and his starting point was sitting
in the back row, her eyes locked with his.

Anticipation crowded the room until it was a
wonder there was still room left for the people.

He stopped at the end of her row, but before he
had time to even consider moving toward her chair,

she was there, meeting him in the aisle, wrapping her arms around his shoulders and neck.

The fifty-some-odd people at this meeting of Romantics Anonymous watched in wonder as Cynthia held on to Lane as if she were clinging to life itself. Then they put their hands together and clapped. The applause was loud and long, and not a soul felt like stopping, not even when the two who were entwined relaxed their hold and, by tacit agreement, moved toward the door.

Chapter Eleven

"If you hadn't come back, do you know what I would have done?"

"I told you I was coming back, Cyn."

"I know. But do you know what I would have done if you hadn't?" Cynthia lifted her head from Lane's shoulder.

They were sitting on a wooden bench in a park about a mile from the R.A. meeting. Lane had his arm around her shoulders.

The breeze was twirling strands of her hair. He pushed them gently from her eyes. "What would you have done?"

She gazed at him a moment, studying his face like it was fine art. His expression was so loving, so strong. And there was a sense of awe, of wonder in his eyes that made her smile because she was feeling it, too.

"I would have come after you." She whispered the words, but no whisper had ever sounded so sure.

A stab of regret dimmed his gaze, regret that she had even considered the possibility that he wouldn't return. "Ah, Cyn—"

She pressed two fingers to his lips and shook her head. "I would have come after you because nothing feels as right as our being together—you, me and Beth." Her fingers moved from his lips to his cheek to his chin, and then down to his chest. "You know, all those years ago I didn't think I could compete with your dreams."

"You don't have to."

"I'm not going to. I want you to have your dreams *and* us. And I want you to know that if you need to live in L.A.—"

This time Lane cut her off. "No." His tone was adamant, but he thanked her with a gentle squeeze. "I like it here."

He drew Cynthia against him and looked around the park. The trees were bare and winter-gray now, but would burst with rich life in the spring. He looked at the swings that were empty and still and knew that the first sunny day would bring children laughing and shrieking as they pumped harder and harder and swung higher and higher. For a moment he had a glimpse of himself and Cynthia, standing behind a small child and taking turns giving pushes. The vision brought a smile to his face. He glanced down and saw that Cynthia had followed his gaze—and most likely his thoughts—and that she was smiling, too.

He placed a whisper-soft kiss on the top of her head and said again, simply, "I love it here with you."

Cynthia wound her arms around his waist. They

were quiet for a time, and then she asked, "You remember the 'Jack Phelpps Show'?" She felt Lane grin against her hair.

"How could I forget? We should introduce Jack to Barbara Atchity. They might hit it off."

Cynthia shook her head. "Not a good idea. Rumor has it they're the same person." She hugged him. "Anyway, you remember what I said about being able to create passion?"

"Yes?" There was a frown in his voice.

Cynthia rubbed her cheek against his chest. "I was wrong. I can't create it." She leaned back to look at him. "You can, though. You create it in me very well...and very often."

Lane cleared his throat and leaned toward her.

"Listen, if you're not doing anything right now, how'd you like to go for a little drive and then... park?"

Cynthia raised her brows at the highly unoriginal suggestion. She glanced around them. "Seems to me that we're already 'parked.' Why waste all that time driving?"

Lane grinned. "You're bad," he growled, drawing her closer. "You're very—" he kissed her softly "—very—" and then more seductively, whispering the last word against her mouth "—bad...."

The days that followed were filled with celebration. There was a wedding to plan and Christmas to prepare for.

Because neither Cynthia nor Lane—nor Beth—could bear the thought of waiting, it was decided by the whole family that the wedding should take place on Christmas Eve.

Lea started baking. Gwen, Cynthia and Beth shopped for Cynthia's dress. Lane grinned like an idiot and tried to convince Cynthia that one year was the perfect duration for a honeymoon.

Through it all, the joy and the hope seemed too great to be contained in one or two bodies alone, and they were all glad they could share it with each other.

Only one concern gnawed at Cynthia, distracting her at times from the fun of the plans, and she knew that this time around, she would best honor her future with Lane by confiding in him.

"My father was here…in Medford, I mean," she said one night without preamble as she and her husband-to-be relaxed by the fireplace in her living room.

He nodded, but said nothing, having heard the news from Gwen, and knowing, too, that Cynthia had felt unable to see her father thus far.

Cynthia was lying next to Lane on the couch. They'd had little time alone the past several days, but they never missed an opportunity to touch or to be near enough to breathe each other's scents or to feel the other person's warmth.

Right now, Lane was sitting back against the arm of the sofa, bolstered by a pillow, with his feet on the floor so there was room for Cynthia to stretch out beside him. His left arm was wrapped around her shoulders; his hand played with a wisp of blond hair and dipped into the curve of her collarbone. The fingers of his right hand were entwined with the fingers of her left in a traditional lovers' clasp, although they hadn't yet had the time or the privacy to share the consummation they both craved.

Beth was upstairs in her room with a friend. The girls were playing with Mario and Luigi and listening to music.

Cynthia rubbed her cheek against Lane's sweater and toyed with his fingers.

"Gwen said he's still in town," she said softly, the words muffled by the wool of his pullover. "I think that before the wedding, I should... I think maybe I'll..."

Lane's arm tightened around her shoulders; his hand squeezed hers. He spoke with his lips buried in her silky hair. "I'll drive you."

"An hour?" Lane asked while the car idled in Park behind them.

Cynthia nodded.

Lane gathered her close for one last bracing hug and looked over her head at the Motel 6. He held her upper arms and gently pushed her away when she seemed ready to burrow inside his coat.

"It's two o'clock on the nose," he said, smiling at her encouragingly and bending forward to plant a kiss on her forehead. "I'll be out here at three. If you want more time, just let me know."

"Okay. I love you." She never tired of saying it, never tired of seeing his eyes warm with pleasure when she did.

He waited for her to walk toward the motel. As she turned the corner, she looked back to see him still standing by the car, and she continued on to room 206 knowing that, no matter what, she had his love to come home to.

She knocked on the orange door. To her own ears, the thumping of her heart sounded louder than her rap on the door. It seemed to Cynthia that her heart had been beating double time since she'd telephoned her father yesterday.

They had agreed to meet here at the motel, and the moment Cynthia was dreading the most was this first one, when they would see each other for the first time in eighteen years.

Their phone conversation had been brief and stilted: "It's me—Cynthia.... I'll meet you tomorrow... 2:00 p.m. is fine.... Yes, Medford has grown.... I'm looking forward to it, too.... Goodbye."

Doubts had assailed her since then. He'd sounded older on the phone, his voice thinner, less robust. She wondered if an hour was too long a period of time to set...or too short? She tortured herself with questions and doubts until the orange motel door swung slowly open.

In one swift, all-encompassing glance, Cynthia noted the brown-and-rust motel bedspread, the permanent depression in the mattress where so many others had slept. She saw two plastic cups and two unopened cans of soda on a table near the window. Then her gaze took in the craggy lines on the face of the aging man before her, the happiness and the gratitude in his twinkling green eyes, and suddenly the first moment took care of itself.

There were, indeed, awkward minutes during the hour that followed. But there were also explanations, avouchments, apologies...and the first halting steps toward forgiveness.

When the hour was up, Henry walked Cynthia to the parking lot.

"I'm getting married on Christmas Eve," Cynthia

said, feeling almost shy about telling a father something he would, under other circumstances, already have known.

Henry's smile was genuine. "Aw, honey, that's great. It's a good night to get married. Lotsa love, new beginnings...."

"I'd like you to be there." She stopped walking as she thought of something. "Oh, but I think I should ask Mother. The wedding's going to be at her place. Nothing fancy, though, just—"

"I don't think I can make it, Cinna—" He started to use the endearment he'd given her years ago, then caught himself shyly, as though he believed he'd relinquished the right to use it. "I'm working that night, honey. Got a gig playing Santa at a retirement home in Eugene. You know, a little magic, a little cheer—nothing fancy, but the old folks seem to like it." His faded green eyes grew anxious. "I'm not sure they could get anybody else this close to Christmas."

Cynthia put her hand on his arm. "It's all right. I understand. You can be there for our first anniversary." It wasn't merely a platitude, and Henry seemed to understand that. They each had a need to make a nebulous future relationship more concrete.

"Next year on Christmas Eve," he said, nodding. "Nothing'll keep me away." They smiled at each other a moment, letting trust build slowly. "Just so's you know, honey," Henry added, "my coming to your wedding would be okay with your mother, I think. She and I had our talk a few days ago."

Cynthia was thankful for that, too. Henry had been as honest as he could be about regretting the way he'd walked out on his family and about being afraid to come back once the damage had been done. He'd spent the last few years traveling the country like he'd always wanted to, but missing the family he'd left behind—and wanting to make it right again.

Lane was waiting in the parking lot when she and Henry rounded the corner of the building. The two men shook hands, and then Cynthia watched her father walk back to the Motel 6.

Chapter Twelve

Christmas Eve day was clear and sparkling both inside the house and out. Lea, Gwen, Beth and Gwen's girls decorated the living room, the stairs, the hallways and the front door with cherubs and plastic wedding bells covered in glitter, and with Christmas elves dancing on strings. Red velvet ribbon wreathed the balustrade. It was sweet, it was sentimental, it was unashamedly romantic.

The wedding was strictly a family affair, but Cynthia primped for it as nervously as if she were going to be seated in the first row at the Academy Awards.

The dress that she, Gwen and Beth had picked out was cream lace from neckline to floor and from shoulder to wrist. It left her long neck bare, and as a woman in love she wasn't too modest to flaunt the aspect she knew Lane admired. She pulled her hair back from her face, secured it with a gold filigree barrette and looped the ponytail back under the clip.

Then, with Beth—her maid of honor—leading the way, Cynthia walked downstairs to her wedding ceremony.

A pair of ocean-green eyes met a pair that were chocolate brown, and a decade melted away in a heartbeat. To the two people who stared at each other like exiles looking toward home, there was no time, no distance, no past in their way.

The brown eyes were older now, with lines radiating out from their corners. The green eyes bore lashes that had thinned a bit through the years. It didn't matter.

Their common gaze was as breathless and deep as it had been those many years ago, when two strangers stood under a tree after P. Anderson's Nineteenth-Century American Poetry class and found shelter.

Rev. Dave Stephenson, who was a neighbor of Milton and Lea's, performed the ceremony at four-forty-five in the afternoon. After a celebratory glass of champagne, he returned to his own home for supper, carrying a plate laden with the wedding cake he would somehow find room to eat—in between the Christmas cookies and candy his wife and congregation supplied.

In the living room of Lea's house, Beth ate cake, drank eggnog and played her tape of the wedding march over and over until Aunt Fanny whipped the tape from the cassette player and replaced it with Dolly Parton. Gwen and Franklin tried to keep their daughters' curious fingers away from the presents stacked underneath the Christmas tree, and Lea and Milton tried a country two-step by the fireplace.

The menorah Franklin had brought with him to celebrate Chanukah glowed brightly with eight freshly lit candles even though Chanukah was over. But Chanukah was a holiday of celebration and miracles and faith, so it seemed fitting to light the candles and let them share their glow with the newlyweds.

Cynthia and Lane leaned against one paneled wall. His right arm was curled securely around her, held snugly by the pressure of her hand pressing his arm to her waist. The fingers of their left hands were linked. With their heads tilted, they stared into each other's eyes, rubbing the wedding rings with their fingers, thinking how wonderful it was to be joined in love and to wear the bands that let the whole world know about it.

"You look mighty fine in that new suit of yours, Mr. Lincoln," Cynthia drawled, matching her accent to Dolly Parton's.

"And you know what that gorgeous dress of yours is doing to me right now, don't you, Mrs. Lincoln?" Lane returned in a low growl.

Cynthia smiled without feigning innocence. "Yes."

Lane grinned down at her. "Hussy."

He bent lower and placed his lips lightly on her ear. His warm breath delighted and tickled her.

"Stop giggling, Mrs. Lincoln." They were using their reinstated titles with the same relentless enthusiasm the children would show their new Christmas toys.

Lane squeezed Cynthia's waist. "I have something important to tell you."

Cynthia stilled. Lane's voice whispered for her ear alone.

"I reserved the Taos suite at the Waterside Inn." He named one of the loveliest bed and breakfasts in Ashland, a town renowned for its romantic and historical inns.

Cynthia swirled in his arms. "Starting when?" she asked breathlessly.

"Starting tonight."

Cynthia immediately began planning their getaway. She was about to grab Lane's hand and lead him upstairs to help him pack, when the doorbell rang.

"I'll get it!" Beth was up and running in the dark-green velvet dress she had worn for the wedding.

"Ask who it is!"

"Look through the peephole!"

Once again, Lane and Cynthia chorused the instructions.

Their daughter complied with their wishes, and a moment later they heard her announce, "It's Santa Claus."

Lane pushed away from the wall and walked swiftly to the foyer. Gwen and Franklin's daughters clamored after him.

Cynthia and the others listened to the rumble of lowered voices, then to the glad, cheery boom of "Ho, ho, ho! Me-e-erry Christmas!"

Shocked, the adults watched a figure garbed in tomato-red stomp into view. Santa Claus.

His baggy jacket and pants were made of worn red velvet. His belt was black patent leather. He wore boots that looked too big for his feet, a red cap from which thick, phony white hair tumbled about his shoulders, and a white beard and mustache. He had fake shaggy eyebrows and carried a large red felt bag.

"Me-e-erry Christmas!"

His voice cracked on the "merry."

Walking into the living room, Santa dropped his bag on the floor and took centre stage. "Is there a little girl named Allison here?"

Allison skipped quickly over to Santa.

"I have something here for you, li'l Allison." He dug into his bag. "Oh-oh, where is it?" He fished around up to his shoulder. "Well, isn't that somethin', I thought it was right here...."

He stood up and looked at Allison quizzically. "Well now, how in the name of Rudolph did your present wind up there?"

He reached behind Allison's neck, under her pretty, wavy hair. When he pulled his hand back, it appeared that he had pulled from her collar a small package wrapped in bright gold foil.

Allison laughed and clapped her hands. Nikki could barely contain herself, running up to Santa for her present and her turn at the magic.

She wasn't disappointed. This time Santa turned the felt bag inside-out looking for the gift. When everyone was convinced that the bag was empty, he righted it again, reached inside and came up with not one but two wrapped boxes—one for Nikki and one for her parents.

Fanny's gift appeared from inside her own pocket.

He pulled Lea and Milton's present from beneath a sofa cushion.

Beth's gift was the first to appear unwrapped. Santa hugged her, a long, tender hug which rocked them gently from side to side. When he pulled away, he held her face in his white-gloved hands.

"You're as lovely as your mother was at your age. You like the snow, young lady?"

"Yes, very much."

"Ah, so did she. So did she." His hands fell away from her face, and he turned to collect his bag.

It was Gwen who noticed the gold angel suspended from a chain around Beth's neck.

As Santa made ready to leave, Allison and Nikki, the souls of fairness, scampered up to him, tugging on his red jacket. He turned around, raising one shaggy eyebrow.

"You forgot Aunt Cynthia and Lane." The whispered attempt to spare Santa any embarrassment was duly noted.

Glancing at the couple just mentioned, Santa frowned and pointed in their direction. "Them, you mean?" he asked, and Allison and Nikki nodded in unison.

Santa stroked his white beard. "So I did, so I did." Then he leaned down and whispered to the girls. "Weren't they just married today?"

Again the heads bobbed.

"Old love and a new start," Santa mused. "Seems to me they got the best gift of all. Is that the bride's bouquet?"

He pointed to the small bouquet of red roses and baby's breath Cynthia had unceremoniously laid on the coffee table. "Mind if I look at it? I haven't seen one of those i: ı long time."

He picked it up in careful, magician's hands, raised it to inhale the fragrance of the roses, then took it to Cynthia and held it out to her. "It suits you."

Although everyone would swear later that all he had done was raise the bouquet to his face, Cynthia glanced down to find something glittering among the blooms. She reached between two roses and extracted a gold medallion and chain. Engraved into the gold was an inscription: "Faith, hope and love…and the greatest of these is love."

When Cynthia raised her head again, Santa was leaving, escorted by two giggling, enthralled little girls. The moment the door shut behind him, chaos ensued with the children begging to be allowed to open their packages now and the adults laughing and arguing over how Santa had put the necklace around Beth's neck without anyone seeing it happen.

Cynthia quietly edged away from the group. By the time she made it to the front porch, "Santa" was preparing to get into his sleigh—a blue Chevy Nova.

The night was clear and black and still. All Cynthia had to do to stop him was call out.

She opened her mouth but no call came. She had assiduously avoided addressing her father during the hour they had spent together. What should she call him now? Santa? Henry?

He got into his car and reached for the door.

"Daddy!"

The man in the cheap, rented costume stood up,

turned, then shut his door softly and walked slowly around the car.

Cynthia met him at the curb.

"The medallion… I… It's beautiful. And the girls were so thrilled. I just wanted… Well, I just wanted to say…"

Henry Gordon James had never known wealth. He'd scraped together every last dime to buy the gifts for tonight. But when he opened his arms and felt his daughter fall into them, he knew there could be no richer man on God's good sweet Earth.

"I love you, Cinnamon Girl," he whispered hoarsely. "I'll be here for your anniversary. And before that, if you'll have me."

For Cynthia, hugging him for a few moments could not replace all the hugs they'd missed through the years. But it was a start. A very, very good start.

It wasn't until after he'd gotten into his Chevy and driven away that she realized how cold it was outside. Hugging her arms to her chest, she turned to walk back to the house. Halfway up the walk she saw Lane waiting for her.

His smile and his eyes asked the question, *Are you all right?*

She smiled back to reassure him, but the smile became a loopy grin which said plainly, *I love you.*

He reached out and drew her toward him, enfolding her in his warming embrace.

"I love you, too. I'll never stop." He whispered the pledge against her temple.

They stood there in the front yard a moment, drinking in the sights and the sounds and the good

smells of the season. Then they walked back together, to a house filled with romance. And to a
future filled with the magic of true love.

*   *   *   *   *

MILLS & BOON®

*M*akes
any time
special

Enjoy a romantic novel from
Mills & Boon®

Presents™ *Enchanted*™ *Temptation*®

Historical Romance™ *Medical Romance*™

MILLS & BOON®

Next Month's Romance Titles

♡

Each month you can choose from a wide variety of romance novels from Mills & Boon®. Below are the new titles to look out for next month from the Presents™ and Enchanted™ series.

Presents™

TO WOO A WIFE	Carole Mortimer
CONTRACT BABY	Lynne Graham
IN BED WITH THE BOSS	Susan Napier
SURRENDER TO SEDUCTION	Robyn Donald
OUTBACK MISTRESS	Lindsay Armstrong
THE SECRET DAUGHTER	Catherine Spencer
THE MARRIAGE ASSIGNMENT	Alison Kelly
WIFE BY AGREEMENT	Kim Lawrence

Enchanted™

BE MY GIRL!	Lucy Gordon
LONESOME COWBOY	Debbie Macomber
A SUITABLE GROOM	Liz Fielding
NEW YEAR...NEW FAMILY	Grace Green
OUTBACK HUSBAND	Jessica Hart
MAKE-BELIEVE MOTHER	Pamela Bauer & Judy Kaye
OH, BABY!	Lauryn Chandler
FOLLOW THAT GROOM!	Christie Ridgway

On sale from 8th January 1999

H1 9812

Available at most branches of WH Smith, Tesco, Asda, Martins, Borders and all good paperback bookshops

MILLS & BOON®

Medical Romance™

COMING NEXT MONTH

SARAH'S GIFT by Caroline Anderson
Audley Memorial Hospital

Having lost her own family, Sarah loved having Matt Ryan
and his little girl, Emily, living with her while they were in
England. She didn't know that Matt had an inestimable
gift for her...

POTENTIAL DADDY by Lucy Clark

Kathryn wasn't sure she liked the professional Jack—brilliant
and arrogant—but his private side was a revelation. He'd
make the perfect father, but who would he choose as the
mother of his potential children?

LET TOMORROW COME by Rebecca Lang

Gerard came to Jan's help when she most needed it, but she
found it so hard to trust, she was sure he'd have a hidden
agenda. How could he convince her that he hadn't?

THE PATIENT MAN by Margaret O'Neill

Harry Paradine knew if he was patient enough that the right
woman would come along. When she finally did, he found
Emily Prince less than trustful—but why?

*Available at most branches of WH Smith, Tesco, Asda,
Martins, Borders, Easons, Volume One/James Thin
and most good paperback bookshops*

LYNN ERICKSON

The Eleventh Hour

Jack Devlin is on Death Row, convicted of murdering his beautiful socialite wife. But the evidence is too cut and dry for lawyer Eve Marchand. When Jack escapes and contacts Eve, she is forced to make a decision that changes her life.

"Lynn Erickson joins the ranks of Sandra Brown and Nora Roberts"

—The Paperback Forum

1-55166-426-7
**AVAILABLE IN PAPERBACK
FROM DECEMBER, 1998**

SHARON
SALA

Tory Lancaster is a woman trying to
leave behind a legacy of abandonment and sorrow.
She is about to come face to face with her past. A past
she must confront if she is to have any
hope of possessing a future.

SWEET
BABY

MIRA®

1-55166-416-X
AVAILABLE IN PAPERBACK
FROM DECEMBER, 1998

LINDA HOWARD

DIAMOND BAY

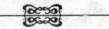

Someone wanted this man dead. He was barely alive as
he floated up to the shore. Shot twice and unconscious.
Rachel's sixth sense told her she was his only hope.
The moment she decided not to call the police
she decided his future. As well as her own.

"Howard's writing is compelling."

—Publishers Weekly

1-55166-307-4
AVAILABLE IN PAPERBACK
FROM DECEMBER, 1998

We are giving away a year's supply of Mills & Boon® books to the five lucky winners of our latest competition. Simply match the six film stars to the films in which they appeared, complete the coupon overleaf and send this entire page to us by 30th June 1999. The first five correct entries will each win a year's subscription to the Mills & Boon series of their choice. What could be easier?

CABARET	_	**GONE WITH THE WIND**	_
ROCKY	_	**SMOKEY & THE BANDIT**	_
PRETTY WOMAN	_	**GHOST**	_

C8L

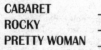

Please turn over for details of how to enter ➜

HOW TO ENTER

There are six famous faces and a list of six films overleaf. Each of the famous faces starred in one of the films listed and all you have to do is match them up!

As you match each one, write the number of the actor or actress who starred in each film in the space provided. When you have matched them all, fill in the coupon below, pop this page in an envelope and post it today. Don't forget you could win a year's supply of Mills & Boon® books—you don't even need to pay for a stamp!